The smoke-wre   es
teetered and fell   e
being shaken. No   n,
thus letting him fa   f
moving with it, pa   -
ing them, flying straight for the swirling, rolling, horrifying
mass of energy just beyond the open portal.

Then, with a mighty boom of sound, he was sucked
through the portal into absolute, terrifying darkness. . . .

RESTORATION

SEAN DALTON

ACE BOOKS, NEW YORK

This book is an Ace original edition,
and has never been previously published.

RESTORATION

An Ace Book / published by arrangement with
the author

PRINTING HISTORY
Ace edition / April 1994

ISBN: 0-441-00034-7

ACE®
Ace Books are published by The Berkley Publishing Group,
200 Madison Avenue, New York, New York 10016.
ACE and the "A" design
are trademarks belonging to Charter Communications, Inc.

PRINTED IN THE UNITED STATES OF AMERICA

10 9 8 7 6 5 4 3 2 1

CHAPTER 1

Noel Kedran shivered in the winter darkness of the unlit alley. The icy winds coming off Lake Michigan sliced down the streets, and stabbed through his protective clothing like a stiletto through paper.

Trojan, his best friend and backup for tonight, was late. Noel checked the time again and cursed to himself. Trojan had promised to be here, after Noel spent several days talking his hairy friend into it. Now Trojan had failed him.

Bitterness welled up in Noel, a sour, raging anger that seemed to catch him without warning more and more frequently of late. He bottled it, knowing that he had to keep his wits about him now. Tonight was his one chance of revenge. He'd worked for twelve weeks for this chance—twelve weeks of dogged searching, bribing snitches, hacking into the police informer networks, and scouting through the roughest parts of the old city to unearth this one particular cell of Anarchists. If they stuck to the typical Anarchist pattern, they would disband the cell soon and re-form elsewhere. If that happened, he'd never again find the individuals who had killed his old mentor Tchielskov and sent Noel spinning into a closed time loop for all eternity.

More shivers wracked him, shivers that had less to do with the bitter Chicago cold than the mess he had become inside. He blamed the Anarchists for that as well. As he stared up at

1

the dingy, second-story apartment where a feeble light glowed around the edges of a blackout curtain, he could feel the shakes grow worse. He didn't have to be asleep for the nightmares to haunt him. Clawing, desperate dreams of scourging lash or howling mobs. Without warning, he would see the lovely faces of women he'd met in those travels to the past, women who bent down to kiss him, then turned abruptly into serpents and struck his lips with their fangs. The poison would fill his mouth, and he'd wake up choking for breath, his hands clawing his throat, his heart racing. In other dreams he stood trapped in a chamber of mirrors, seeing his reflection no matter which way he turned, a reflection that jeered and cursed him as it grew progressively distorted.

"Leon," he whispered aloud, while his hands trembled uncontrollably and the hatred inside him burned like acid.

The Anarchists had done that to him as well, had saddled him with a mirror image, a duplicate copied from him during his plunge through the time stream. Leon was a complete reversal of Noel—from his name to his personality. Noel was left-handed; Leon was right-handed. Noel believed in the purpose of the Time Institute, which was to bring mankind back to the virtues of courage, honor, and valor by witnessing and recording examples from the past. Leon's conscience was nonexistent. If he wasn't trying to destroy Noel, he was busy trying to destroy history.

And yet, Leon—despicable, cowardly, scheming—was more than a blurred copy. Leon was a part of Noel, a part he did not want to admit.

He would never forgive the Anarchists for bringing him face-to-face with that side of himself. Never.

Above him the dim light went out. Noel crouched lower in the shadows, his entire body tensed. The meeting was over. The Anarchists would be slipping out one by one to the landing. They would go down the rusted, ancient fire escape like shadows.

He was mature enough to know that revenge was never all it promised. Revenge couldn't undo what had happened, couldn't bring Tchielskov back to life, couldn't take the nightmares away, couldn't find Leon where he still romped unchecked in the past. The shrinks at the Institute had talked to Noel long and hard about the futility of tracking down those who had hurt him. But revenge was what he wanted, and what he meant to have.

Noel reached beneath his jacket and pulled out a Fabrio 94. It was a very illegal weapon, bought off the black market yesterday, its modern heft and shape alien to his hands, which had been trained to use the ancient weapons of sword, dagger, and bow. This gun had laser sights, loose-jacketed ammunition with homing sensors, and aim-tracking assist. It was a powerful and deadly weapon, one favored by Anarchists. The irony of that appealed to him. He would pick them off one by one as they came down the fire escape, and they would die in silence in the darkness.

A hand closed upon his shoulder from behind. Noel jerked in alarm and nearly fired the weapon.

"Easy!" rumbled Trojan's deep voice in his ear.

The wild hammering inside Noel eased off. He gulped in a breath and barely stopped himself from jabbing the Fabrio's muzzle into Trojan's chest.

"You took your sweet time!" he whispered angrily. "They're coming out."

Above, at the window, there was a slight flutter of movement. The curtain slid aside, and a shadowy figure appeared in silhouette.

"I was in a briefing," murmured Trojan. "Couldn't get away until late. Sorry."

Aflare with fresh resentment, Noel turned his head away. Briefings meant travel, something denied to him now. He didn't want to be angry with Trojan, but his friend still had access to a world and all its wondrous events that was now closed to Noel. It had placed a rift between them, a rift Trojan tried to ignore, but Noel couldn't.

He wished suddenly that he hadn't asked Trojan to help him tonight. He knew the feeling was unfair, but he went on feeling it anyway.

The first Anarchist had emerged now on the landing. He was cloaked in a night suit, a special fabric that absorbed almost one hundred percent of the light spectrum and made its wearer practically invisible. Raising the weapon, Noel squinted through the sights, which were calibrated in compensation, and found his target.

He held his breath and started squeezing the trigger.

Trojan's powerful hand clamped hard around his wrist and pulled the gun down.

Furious, Noel tried to wrestle free. "Damn you!" he breathed. "What are you doing?"

"Since when did you become an assassin?" retorted Trojan, equally quietly. "Where's the honor in shooting them in the back?"

The first Anarchist was nearly to the ground, his weight on the ancient ladder making the metal squeak and groan. A second Anarchist had started down, and the third and last member of the cell stood on the landing. In seconds they would be gone. Noel went wild inside, but Trojan's muscular arm was clamped around him like a vise. Struggling would give their presence away; Noel could do nothing.

He relaxed in Trojan's hold, his muscles aching from the strain to break free. Sweat had broken out on his face. He could feel time passing with every heartbeat, and his sense of urgency increased. He should have known Trojan would betray him. He should have done this alone.

"Back off," he whispered. "I—"

Trojan's other hand was still clamped on his wrist. The pressure there was intolerable, as though Trojan meant to crush his bones. Noel gritted his teeth against the pain. Trojan shook his arm, trying to make him drop the gun. But Noel hung on. Had Trojan become an Anarchist sympathizer? The very suspicion was infuriating. Noel hit him with his free fist, the blow thudding into solid muscle and numbing his hand. Trojan increased the pressure, and Noel felt his fingers losing circulation, losing the grip that was so vital.

The first Anarchist was on the ground, hurrying away. Noel reared up.

"No!" he shouted, and his voice echoed off the alley walls.

He pulled the trigger, although Trojan had the gun's muzzle aimed at the sky. There was a muted flash, and the Fabrio recoiled against Noel's palm. The shot went nowhere, wasted.

With shouts, the Anarchists scattered.

Trojan heaved Noel to his feet. "Come on! Now it's fair."

Noel wrenched free at last, so furious it was all he could do not to shoot Trojan. "You idiot! You've let them—"

One of the Anarchists shot back, and fire scorched Noel's arm. He twisted and went down, his left side awash with agony, his body barely registering the impact with the ground.

Trojan rolled to the other side of the alley and dived for cover behind a pile of frozen garbage.

Overcoming the pain that had him gasping and writhing, Noel raised up on his good elbow and aimed at the third figure now scrambling back up the fire escape. The Fabrio bucked in his hand, and the Anarchist screamed and fell.

Another shot whizzed by Noel's head. He ducked.

Across the alley, Trojan let out a bloodcurdling war cry and threw a dagger, which thunked solidly into its intended target.

He ran forward, yelling, "Last one is yours, my friend!"

Noel's earlier fury faded, and he had to grin at his crazy friend. Trojan's insistence on fighting with medieval tactics in the middle of the twenty-sixth century spoke of his commitment to old-fashioned valor.

The one remaining Anarchist had given up fighting. He ran full tilt up the alley. In seconds he would be out on State Street, lost forever in the confusion and jostle of the Red Booth District.

Noel scrambled to his feet and lurched into a run after him. The Fabrio had a very limited range. He had to get closer before he could fire again. He had to get his target while they were both still in the alley.

As he ran he kept one eye on the distance counter on the side of the gun. When it started flashing acquisition range, Noel sucked in a deep breath and raised the weapon. It wasn't even necessary to stop and assume a shooter's stance. All he had to do was aim and fire, and the homing sensors would zero in on his target.

Just as he squeezed the trigger, however, the ground vanished beneath his feet. The distant glow of the streetlights zoomed at him, and the alley walls twisted as though they would fall on him. He felt intense pain, as though his body were being turned inside out, then he fell and hit solid ground with a thud that wrung a grunt from him.

The blinding lights receded, and the walls straightened back to where they belonged. Noel lay there, gasping for breath, and tasted the sickly sweetness of blood. Alarms wailed in the distance.

Footsteps came running, then Trojan was kneeling over him. "Noel! Are you all right?"

His hands gripped the back of Noel's jacket and pulled him up. Noel blinked hard, trying to bring himself back into focus. He stared up into the worried face of his friend. Craggy of feature, built like a slab of rock, and covered with a pelt of red hair, Trojan Heitz was a man designed for another century. He was as solid and loyal as they came. Noel was ashamed that he'd doubted Trojan even for a moment.

Noel spat out a mouthful of blood. "What was that?" he asked thickly.

Trojan's nose was bleeding, and he wiped it impatiently. "Are you shot? Did you fall? What happened? You missed him, you know."

Scowling, Noel worked his tongue busily around his teeth in search of a loose one. They all seemed solidly attached. He spat out more blood and pulled himself up with Trojan's help. A moment of dizziness made him sway, then he straightened and shook off Trojan's supporting hand.

"I'm okay. Now. I think." Noel put a hand to his head for a moment, trying to work it out. "That was a doozy. I've heard about them in theory, of course, but—"

Trojan took his arm again. "You'd better sit down."

Noel shook him off. "Quit grabbing me. I'm fine. How about you?"

"You're the one not making any sense. Aha, you *are* shot. I figured as much when you fell down."

"I didn't fall down," said Noel impatiently. Trojan probed his forearm, and Noel winced. "Leave it alone. It's a graze. The distortion is more important."

"What distortion?"

Noel stared up into his friend's puzzled eyes, and his own frustration grew. "The *distortion*. You know, a few seconds ago, when the world turned inside out?"

Trojan snorted. "You were shot, and you fell down. That's all, Noel. Let's not get dramatic."

"Dramatic?" Noel heard himself shouting, but he didn't care. He couldn't believe Trojan was shrugging this off. "Do you know how rare a time distortion is? Do you know how unlikely? Do you know how dangerous?"

"Of course I know. Calm down, and let's get out of here before those sirens come any closer. I want to recover my dagger. If it's traced to the Institute, Dr. Rugle will—"

"You're not listening to me," said Noel through gritted teeth. He followed Trojan down the alley, clutching his wounded arm and feeling increasingly baffled. "Didn't you experience it?"

"Experience what?"

"The distortion!"

Behind them an air shuttle swept over State Street, its searchlight stabbing down. Trojan glanced over his shoulder. "Quick. Let's get out of here."

They paused only to recover Trojan's dagger, then ran from the alley into the warren of shadowy streets beyond. Minutes later, Noel wiped down the Fabrio and tossed it into the river. They stood at the bridge, and Noel felt a fresh series of shivers go through him. He was getting light-headed from delayed reaction, while Trojan seemed to have suffered no ill effects at all, other than the nosebleed, which had stopped.

"Killing makes a bad night's work," said Trojan moodily. "Let's go home."

"Home?" said Noel in surprise. "But don't you think we should report to the Institute?"

"Why? Do you intend to confess your—"

"Trojan, will you cut this? A time distortion is serious. You can't ignore it. Rugle will have the whole Institute on alert—"

"Hold it," said Trojan firmly. His blue eyes caught Noel's. "You must—"

"Trojan, I'm telling you, it—"

"Noel! Calm down."

"How can I calm down? The time fabric has pulled apart. There's trouble. Do I have to spell it out? Leon has probably changed history. Our present could be ending right now. We—"

"Nothing is ending," said Trojan firmly. He gripped Noel by the shoulders and shook him. "Nothing! Listen to me."

"No, you listen to me," said Noel urgently. "I experienced it. And you did, too, only you won't admit it."

"Nothing happened, my friend," said Trojan.

The gentleness in his tone sent Noel's blood boiling. "Don't try to humor me, damn you!"

"I'm not humoring you. I'm trying to get you home so we can treat that arm. You're going into shock, and we're both going to freeze to death if we stay out here all night."

He tugged at Noel, but Noel planted his feet and didn't budge. "I don't get this. Are you telling me you didn't feel the distortion?"

Trojan emitted a gusty sigh. "Exactly. It didn't happen."

"But it *did*! I fell right through it. And you . . . you must have. Your nose was bleeding."

"That's because I banged it when I dived for cover during the shooting," said Trojan.

Noel frowned, and for a moment he was shaken into doubting himself. Maybe Trojan was right. Maybe it hadn't happened.

"No," he said firmly, squaring his shoulders. "I'm not crazy. Maybe it was tiny. Maybe it only happened to me. Maybe whatever Leon's doing back in the seventeenth century is only going to affect me. I—"

"Noel!" said Trojan in concern. "Stop it. He's gone. He cannot hurt you. He cannot affect you."

"But he's still back there!" cried Noel. "The instruments can track him."

"It's a shadow. The technicians have gone into that again and again. There's a tiny bit of essence still left in the time stream, but not enough to matter. He can't be tangible, Noel. He can't affect anything. He probably isn't corporeal. If he were, history would have changed by now. Think about it. How many times did he try to change things, and you were always there to make the save. Weren't you?"

Noel shrugged. He kept his gaze turned stubbornly on the Chicago River, flowing oily black beneath the reflection of streetlights.

"Nothing has changed," said Trojan persuasively. "We're still here. There's been plenty of time for him to make a difference if he was going to. But he can't. He's gone. He's smoke. There isn't even enough of him to suffer. You're back, and you're whole. That's all that matters."

Noel felt the old fear uncoil inside him, a fear that told him every assurance Trojan offered was false. They could postulate their theories forever, but still Noel knew that Leon continued to exist . . . somewhere . . . back there.

He curled his fingers around the cold steel railing of the bridge. "I'm not whole," he whispered, his voice catching on emotions he didn't want to reveal. "They won't let me travel."

Trojan sighed. After a moment's hesitation, he gripped Noel's shoulder. "You'll be certified fit one of these days. It hasn't been long enough."

Noel whipped his head around and glared at his friend. "And how many weeks will it take? How many months? How many years? They don't trust me. They'll never trust me again."

"They will," said Trojan with conviction. "You're too damned impatient. You always want things to happen immediately. The hag is too cautious for you, but it's her job to be careful."

Noel frowned. Part of him knew that Trojan was right. But the rest of him had to believe his own instincts. "You're traveling soon, aren't you? The briefing that made you late tonight—"

Trojan dropped his gaze away. "I travel tomorrow."

It came back, the resentment, sour and burning in Noel's throat until he could barely contain it. His hands shook, no matter how hard he gripped the railing. But beyond that, a new worry reared its head.

"You can't," said Noel unsteadily, keeping his gaze away from Trojan so as not to betray too much. "It's not safe."

"Noel, don't get started on that again. You've been obsessed with tracking down these Anarchists. You've worked way too hard to find them. But now that's done. You succeeded. You got the creeps who killed Tchielskov."

Noel swallowed hard, letting himself be diverted for a moment. "Most of them."

"One got away. He's gone. You won't find him again."

"I know."

"You have to accept that."

Noel nodded. "I do."

"You did your best."

"Yeah, with your help."

Trojan hesitated. "I had to even the odds, my friend."

Noel looked him dead in the eyes then. "For a moment there I thought you were on their side."

A trace of anger smoldered in Trojan's blue gaze for a moment, then vanished. "Never."

"Yeah," said Noel. "Sorry."

"I wanted you to be able to live with yourself in the morning."

"They're scum! They don't deserve—"

Trojan held up his hand. "No, but *you* deserve a clear conscience. There is justice, and then there is selling your soul for expediency. You know what I'm talking about. Do I have to explain it further?"

"No," whispered Noel, and felt the shame of what he'd nearly done. "Thanks."

"You're welcome. Now, it's late and I'm freezing. I want some coffee to warm me up. We'll go to my place."

"Thanks, but I'd better head across the lake."

Trojan shook his head as though in exasperation, but his smile was kind. "That dump you call home is too far away. Shuttle traffic will be jamming up at this hour for the next work shift. You come home with me and stay tonight."

"I don't need a nursemaid," snapped Noel.

"A drinking companion, maybe?" suggested Trojan slyly.

Noel's annoyance softened. Maybe, if he got Trojan good and drunk, his friend wouldn't be certified to travel tomorrow. That would give Noel time to talk to the technicians about the distortion. He looked at his friend and finally grinned. "Yeah, now that's the best idea you've had all night. Let's go."

CHAPTER 2

∞

Chicago Work Complex 7 was an edifice of bronzed steel and glass sprawling over multiple acres of prime west-side real estate. It held the offices of sixty-two international corporations, a promenade of retail shops and restaurants, three hotels, several theaters, fourteen banks, the Museum of Political/Social History, the Library of Antiquities, and the Time Institute.

An international science symposium on mutations of aquatic single-celled life-forms was being conducted at one of the hotels. Marine biologists, salt tanned and chattering, filled the escalators and slidewalks, hurried past office workers dreamily spaced out on their Life-design head chips, and jammed the lifts.

"Come on, fella!" one called to Noel, holding open the door and waving to him. "There's room to squeeze you in!"

Noel, his head aching from a brandy hangover, his mouth sour from the aftertaste of painkillers, and his arm sore no matter which way he held it, smiled a no-thanks. Normally he would have sprung for the lift. Today, however, he preferred to glide slowly along among the cattle, quiet and complacent, their smiles serene, their eyes slightly blanked out as they enjoyed the fantasies playing inside their heads. But he was late. He'd gotten drunk last night instead of Trojan, and his friend had already left for work when Noel woke up this morning.

"Come on! We'll make room."

"Yeah! Come on."

With a wince Noel stepped onto the lift. As soon as the doors closed scant inches from his nose, he found himself boxed in with a jostling, good-natured crowd of chatterers and back slappers.

"I tell you, Froether's lecture is the one to catch."

"Froether! He's a complete bore. Nothing new since—"

"What about the wonder child? Kefinsky's prodigy? Her paper's at thirteen-hundred hours."

"Yeah? I hear she's got legs like—"

"Fifth floor, please," said Noel quietly. His head gonged from the noise.

"Fifth?" said the woman beside him. Sturdy of build, she had a pleasant, weathered face and sea-colored eyes. "That's the Time Institute, isn't it?"

He didn't want to talk, but nodding tended to make his head fall off. Noel squinted at her, since the soft lights inside the lift hurt his eyes, and said, "That's right."

Intelligent interest filled her expression. "You're a traveler?"

Anger filled him, and he fought the urge to snap at her. After all, she was just making conversation. "Historian," he said, and forced out half a smile.

"I've spent my life on the sea," she said. "I've always wondered what it would be like to see tall ships under sail."

In Noel's ears came the distant roar of cannon fire. For an instant he once again felt a wooden deck yawing beneath his bare feet. The wind singing through the spars, and the sweet-salty scent of the sea ripe in his nostrils. Canvas unfurling with great snaps, shaking free and white in the sunshine, billowing into a cloud as it caught the wind, and the unexpected surge forward as the ship leaped through the waves.

She touched his sleeve, bringing him back from his memories. "You've been there, traveled there, haven't you? I see it in your eyes. You know what it's like."

Noel dropped his gaze from hers. He knew, all right. Just before the technicians at the Institute had managed to finally rescue him from the time loop where he'd been trapped, he'd been on board a pirate vessel in the Caribbean. But travelers weren't allowed to talk about their assignments for security purposes.

Once again he forced a smile for her. "You should come by the library and see a recording."

"In a sensory booth?" She snorted. "It's not the same."

"It's very close."

Politeness dropped across her face. "Perhaps. I'm very busy at this symposium."

"The chance of a lifetime," said Noel, knowing he'd handled the conversation all wrong. One of the primary purposes of the Institute was to keep alive people's interest in history. "If you'll step off with me, I'll get you a pass."

She shook her head. "Thanks, perhaps later. I have a paper to deliver."

"Nils Borgsten is our seafaring expert. If he's in, perhaps you'd like to meet him and take an informal tour of the museum behind the scenes."

Her gaze snapped up, keen again. "Dolphins?" she asked in a whisper, quivering with suppressed excitement. The lift doors opened and she stepped off ahead of Noel.

"Clara, we'll be late," said one of the scientists.

She waved absently at her companions. "I'll catch the next lift."

As soon as the doors closed, she gripped Noel's arm. "Dolphins?" she whispered, her voice almost squeaking in excitement. "Twentieth-century, non-extinct dolphins? Could this Borgsten provide me with data on them?"

"I'm sure—"

"I mean, I've combed through all the research documented at that time. It's threadbare. There's nothing left to do any kind of fresh study on. But something new. Some small fact that hasn't been pawed to death . . . I could finish my dissertation and—"

"How about nineteenth-century dolphins?" asked Noel with a smile. "Or—"

Her grip tightened on his sleeve. "Could you?"

Still smiling, Noel gently disengaged himself from her grip and walked over to the security desk. He explained the situation and asked for Borgsten to be paged.

"He'll be here in a few minutes," said Noel, returning to the woman. "If he can't answer your questions, he can find someone else for you to ask."

"Thank you. I—"

"Excuse me," said Noel. "I'm late for a meeting."

Leaving her glowing with gratitude and excitement, Noel cleared himself through the stringent security checks and headed down the corridor into the depths of the Institute. At the last check-in point, he entered his name into the computer and found several messages waiting for him. The order to report to Dr. Rugle's office had priority.

Noel frowned. He wanted to talk to the hag, all right, but not until he'd had a chance to see Bruthe down in the labs. He tried calling the technician, but the line was blocked.

"No communications permitted to Time Control Access Area," intoned the computer.

Noel's frown deepened, and he felt a spurt of alarm. That meant the time stream was open. They were sending people out. But they couldn't! Not until that distortion he'd encountered was checked out.

With an oath, he grabbed his security badge and headed down the corridor at a run.

Laboratory 14 was bolted shut, with NO ACCESS flashing above the door. Noel hammered on it with his fists, cursing himself for having overslept, cursing Trojan for slipping medication in his cup, cursing himself for not having gotten here sooner.

"Kedran!" said a sharp voice. "Have you gone mad?"

Noel turned, breathless and shaken, to find fellow historian Rupeet staring at him in astonishment and censure. "Has Trojan traveled yet?" Noel demanded.

"How on earth should I know that?"

Noel gripped his arm. "Are you traveling today?"

"I'm scheduled to go at fourteen hundred hours this afternoon—"

"Then you were at last night's briefing."

"Yes, of course I was. Unlike some people, I never miss a prep—"

"Shut up," said Noel, in no mood for Rupeet's snide needling. "If you were at the briefing, then you should know Trojan's schedule."

Rupeet lifted his slim dark brows and pulled free of Noel's grip. "I'm surprised he didn't tell you. You're as thick as thieves, the pair of you, always violating the rules as though this entire operation were some kind of game."

Noel gritted his teeth. "Look, never mind the lecture. Just tell me if he's traveled yet."

"If you haven't been informed, and I see no reason why you should have access to travel schedules, then it's hardly my place to tell you anything," said Rupeet.

"Damn you! There was a distortion last night. The time stream has an instability that needs to be investigated before any of you go out there—"

"Nonsense," snapped Rupeet. "There's been nothing of the kind or it would have been announced. The technicians have aborted none of the missions, and they are exceedingly careful about that sort of thing. Are you certain your holographic implants aren't playing tricks on you, Kedran?"

"I don't have any head chips," growled Noel. "You know that."

"I know nothing of the kind. All I see is someone either mad or on something. You're a disgrace to this—"

"Oh, shut up," said Noel, and hurried away.

He should have known he'd get no answers from Rupeet. The man was an idiot, obsessive about unimportant details, an unimaginative perfectionist who ratted on other people's mistakes and was oblivious to the finer points of experiencing life in the past. His recordings were mundane, boring, petty examinations of minor events. Rupeet could spend hours recording an herbalist grinding potions while outside the garden walls the entire castle might be under siege, and he would never stop to go after the larger event because it would mean upsetting the meticulous organization of his assignment. Why Rugle put up with him, Noel had no idea. Trojan had once attempted to explain to him that Rupeet was dependable and steady, and Rugle could be sure that he'd always come back with what he'd been sent to learn. But Noel had no patience with that. When he'd traveled to the past, he'd left himself open to anything taking place around him. Sometimes it didn't pan out, but he'd returned many times with gems of information that no one else would have dared try for. Noel knew that risks were often necessary, and he'd never hesitated to take them.

Until the Anarchists had sabotaged his Light Operated Computer and trapped him in time. Now that he was back, his wings had been clipped. He was shut out, excluded from the

mission briefings, denied travel, kept busy with debriefings of
his experiences and cataloging his recordings. He was going
crazy shuffling through the library racks, crazy with inactivity,
crazy with wondering if he'd ever be certified to visit the
past again.

Almost as though he could hear Trojan's deep voice rum-
bling over his shoulder came the thought: *How will they ever
think you're stable if you run around the place like a wild
man, claiming distortions that even the Time Computer didn't
register?*

Noel's hurried stride slowed to a walk. He dragged in several deep breaths, evading the curious glances of some of his
co-workers, and ducked into a lavatory to check his appearance. The mirror showed a slight, wiry figure in a technocrat's
knit trouser suit, shaven and unexceptional, except for a slight
wildness about the eyes and the ravaged look of a bad night's
sleep.

He splashed water on his face and combed his black hair,
then headed for Dr. Rugle's office. Perhaps she would listen,
if he expressed himself in bureaucratic terminology and didn't
get upset.

The minute he walked into her office, however, he knew
nothing was going to work. The hag was seated at her large
desk. It was stacked with files, her computer station flashing
data, her headphones filtering additional information to her
brain, a newscast crawling across one wall of her office, and
the useless white noise of ocean waves coming in over the
audio speakers in the ceiling. She wore a brown knit suit that
made her skin look yellow, and only the fabulous string of
pearls which Noel had brought to her from the pirate's trove
made her look the least bit human.

"You're late," she said when he walked in.

Noel thought of several hasty excuses and rejected them. "I
overslept. Bad night."

She snorted and went on working at her computer terminal.
It flashed amber light across her ugly face, making her look
like a troll crouched over a forge.

"Mr. Kedran," she said sharply, looking up as though she'd
caught that unflattering thought, "you purposely ambushed
those individuals last night and killed them. The police have
been here, making inquiries, which I have had to thwart."

"I, uh—"

"I advise you to remain on these premises for the next several days. Morven will assign you quarters here. It was necessary to say that you were on assignment, and therefore unavailable for questioning. See that you keep yourself restricted until further notice."

"Yes, Dr. Rugle."

"Tchielskov was a traitor, Mr. Kedran," she continued in that flat, relentless voice. "A traitor to the Institute and all it stands for, a traitor to society, and a traitor to your friendship with him."

"Those bastards coerced him—"

"No one can be coerced unless he is weak enough to allow it." Her gaze held Noel's without wavering. "Tchielskov could have sabotaged any of eight LOCs that day. He chose yours. I think it's time you forced yourself to deal with that."

Noel grimaced and turned away, jamming his hands deep into his pockets. He didn't need this, didn't need what she was churning up inside him, didn't need confusion now when there were more important things at stake. But at the same time, he decided then and there to clam up about the time distortion. It hadn't registered on the equipment, which meant it couldn't have happened, which meant he must have had a seizure or something, which meant if he went on talking about it they would put him in a rubber room and never let him out.

"He, uh, he must have picked my LOC at random," said Noel unwillingly.

"The tapes show differently. You've seen them, I know, because I asked the psychiatrist to show them to you at your last session."

Angered, Noel swung around to stare at her.

She met his glare coolly. "I think you've been coddled long enough, Mr. Kedran. Tchielskov was your mentor when you were in training. He taught you a great deal. He saw in you what others did not, and he polished a diamond from the rough with considerable patience and hard work. You became one of our best travelers."

She paused there and almost smiled. "Does that surprise you when I say that?"

His glare shifted to the stacks of data disks on her desk. "I guess it does. Praise isn't lavish around here."

Her blunt-fingered hand strayed upward to touch the pearl necklace. Then she dropped her hand to her lap. "I don't know why he sabotaged you, but it was a specific choice. Perhaps he thought you would be the best equipped to survive. Perhaps he had other, less admirable motives. The fact is, you were betrayed by him. Avenging him was a futile gesture. He is not worthy of the risk you took last night, or of the danger you placed Mr. Heitz in."

Noel frowned and turned his back to her, pacing to the far side of her office, then back again. If she was trying to mess him up inside, she was doing a damned good job of it. He'd already asked himself the same questions. Why had Tchielskov done it? Why? And there was never going to be an answer.

"It had to be done, for the Institute if not for the old man," he said harshly. "The Anarchists understand a counterstrike. They thought we couldn't track them down, and now they know differently. They'll think twice before they try to infiltrate us again."

"I see," she said coldly. "You're going to continue to delude yourself. Very well. Then I have no choice but to—"

"What is all this?" he broke in heatedly. "Another test? Is this another reason to keep me kicking my heels around here? When do I get another assignment? When am I going to—"

"When are you going to stabilize?" she said.

He felt like he'd been punched in the stomach. He backed up a step, frowned, and couldn't find anything to say. "I . . . am. I need to work and get over this—"

"You're still frightened of reentering the time stream," she said without mercy. "Don't deny it. The analysts have verified that."

"Well, wouldn't you be?" he retorted, stung.

"It's quite understandable." She paused a moment, then her expression softened. "Why don't you sit down, Noel, and stop looking like that. I'm not trying to wound your ego. I want you to face facts, cope with them, and progress onward."

He looked at the chair she indicated and massaged the tense muscles at the back of his neck. Inside, he was starting to boil. It was bad enough going through one of these sessions with the shrink, but for his own boss to try amateur probing was too much. Still, he couldn't tell her off, not if he wanted to keep his job . . . not if he ever wanted to travel again.

With a sigh he swung around and dropped into the chair. "Look, let me travel again. It's like getting on a horse after you've fallen off. I've got to face the time stream, go through it, and come back. Then I'll know I'm all right."

She shook her head and even managed to look almost regretful. "I'm sorry. That kind of casual solution won't work with the time stream. You can't fear it. Not the kind of fear that's inside you. It would keep you from focusing. It would interfere with your LOC and cause . . . no, you have to work through your problems independently of the time stream. Then you can return."

He didn't believe her. "And how am I going to convince you I'm ready?"

"When you stop having nightmares. When you stop interfering with Bruthe's work by having him track your nonexistent counterpart. When you stop babbling about time distortions that haven't occurred."

Noel shot to his feet, all his good intentions shattered. "How the hell—"

"Mr. Heitz reported your observations of last night before he left on assignment this morning. He said you would be coming in later to file a report, and he wanted his support on record." She also rose to her feet, calm against his anger. "And you made quite a spectacle of yourself upon arrival, running down to Laboratory 14 and trying to enter when the time portal was engaged."

Chagrined, Noel thought of his argument with Rupeet in the corridor. There were surveillance cameras in the ceiling. He always forgot about them. And even if they weren't working, Rupeet would have lost no time in filing a complaint.

Noel set his jaw. "I'm not crazy," he said. "There was a distortion. I don't care if no one else felt it. I don't care if it didn't register on the equipment. There's something wrong with the time fabric. Maybe only for me. Maybe for no one else. But I don't believe that."

"Exactly how far from you was Mr. Heitz when the distortion occurred?"

Her question heartened him for a moment. Maybe she did believe him. Maybe something had registered that they weren't telling yet.

He said, "About thirty yards, forty perhaps. I was running when it happened."

"Mr. Heitz said you were shot and fell."

"No. I was shot earlier. While I was chasing the Anarchist, the distortion caught me. I ran right into it. When it faded, I fell, and the Anarchist escaped. It must have happened in seconds. I'm not sure."

She cocked her head to one side. "Time distortions are theoretical only. We know they are caused when two travelers attempt to visit the same point of time. We believe they may be caused when—"

"When there is a disruption in the time stream, or if an anomaly causes the time fabric to shred."

"Not very precise terminology, Mr. Kedran."

"Never mind about how I phrase it!" he said. "The anomaly is Leon. It has to be. We left him back there, where he doesn't belong."

"Leon is at best a ghost, to use the imprecise definitions of the past," she said impatiently. "This duplication has no physical substance. There are a few particles left in the time stream, but no actual entity remains. Why do you refuse to accept that?"

Noel thumped his chest. "Because in here I know differently."

"Oh, a hunch. Really!"

"Yes, really!" he retorted. "He's not just a duplication. He's part of me. You didn't get all of me back. And it's causing the stream to split. The two of us, separated, are pulling it apart."

She slammed her hand down upon a stack of files. "This is ludicrous. You are postulating hypotheses without any scientific basis whatsoever."

"I don't need a rationale—"

"I do, however. This institute is run on sound scientific principles, not harebrained guesses. You are letting your paranoia consume you. You are becoming irrational."

He glared at her. "Is that a professional opinion, Dr. Rugle?"

She turned bright red. "You will report to Morven now, and be assigned to quarters. You will go to them and remain there until further notice."

"This isn't the military. I can quit."

"You can," she said icily. "But until the police have terminated their investigation into the incident of last night, you will remain here at the Institute, in the quarters assigned to you. Once that matter has been resolved and no substantiated connection is traced to the Institute, then we can determine whether it is desirable to sustain your employment here."

There was nothing left to say. A pulse throbbed in his head. His hands were shaking so hard he clenched them at his sides. Noel turned and strode out so fast the door barely opened quickly enough.

As he paused for it, he bumped the doorway with his shoulder, and his shoulder passed right through solid matter into nothing. Even as he cried out in surprise, the corridor lights rushed at him, blinding him, and the corridor itself twisted around him in a knot. For an instant he was nowhere at all, then he heard screaming and confusion and the rush of thousands of office workers and marine biologists trampling each other in a stampede to escape the building that was falling down upon them. Noel hurtled down several stories, falling with the debris of ceiling tiles, twisted metal, and broken wires. He was falling and falling, tumbling past the waterfall in the reception lobby of the complex. His screams mingled with the tortured groan of metal sheering apart.

He fell forever, then he hit and shattered and came to all at once, finding himself on the floor in the corridor with the alarm shrieking and people surrounding him. The lights were too bright. The sounds were too loud. He winced and tried to put his hand over his face to shield his eyes.

"Everyone, stand back," said a voice of authority. Something sharp pricked his arm, and it all faded.

CHAPTER 3

Noel came out of sedation fighting mad. He sat up on the infirmary cot with a flurry of blankets.

"Hey, hold on there," said a soft voice. Dr. Ellis, as beautiful as she was competent, hurried over just in time to stop him from getting out of bed. "You stay right where you are."

"The hell I will," said Noel. "What's happened? How long have I been out? Who knocked me out?"

She smiled and tilted her head to one side. "Which question do you want me to answer first?"

Her own serene, unruffled manner calmed him down. He drew in a deep breath and felt some of the tension relax in his body. His face was wet with sweat and he wiped it with the sheet. At least he still had his clothes on, which meant they didn't intend a long stay for him. That was a relief. When he'd first opened his eyes to these white, sterile surroundings, he'd been afraid he was already in the rubber room.

"How long?" he said.

"You've been unconscious for four hours, more or less. The sedative was very mild, but I guess your body needed the rest."

He scowled and swung his feet to the floor.

"I don't want you to get up just yet," she said, and her tone was a bit sharper than before. "I'd like to check you out first."

"Why?" he snapped. "Have I been screaming at spiders on the walls?"

"No."

"Did Dr. Rugle order you to keep me here?"

"No."

He glared at her, feeling the wildness clawing up inside him. "I'm not crazy. I'm not!"

She put her hand on his shoulder in quick reassurance. "The distortion registered. We all felt the walls shake. It was a strange, very disconcerting experience."

Noel looked up into her eyes, searching for the truth or a trick. What he saw in her gaze convinced him that she was telling the truth. His nagging fear vanished. With a soft moan, he slumped and buried his face in his hands.

"The lab people are outside clamoring for a chance to get at you," she said after a few moments. "I'd like to keep you here a while longer until I'm sure you feel up to facing them."

"What do they want?" asked Noel.

"Can't you guess?"

He sighed and dropped his hands. "Questions. Like I've got all the answers."

"Don't you?" she said, but with a smile. Her hand slipped from his shoulder to his throat. It could have been a caress, but he felt her fingers upon his pulse, and loosed a mental sigh. That was Angela Ellis. She looked and acted like a peach, but her mind was all business.

"What?" he said belatedly.

"Don't you have all the answers?"

He frowned and pulled away. "No."

"It was just a rhetorical question. If you don't make an effort to relax, I'll have to give you another shot."

He looked up to see if she was teasing and decided she wasn't. "Okay," he said, running his hands through his hair. "I'll relax. Just keep them out for a while."

"I get you first," she said in a sultry voice, but it was a medical scanner she ran over him. "Hold still."

He sat on his hands to hide the tremors. He was beginning to see them as a warning sign of a coming distortion, and he didn't want to go through another one. The last had been a little too real for his peace of mind.

"How about the travelers who were out?" he asked. "Everyone back okay by now? I mean, they didn't send out Rupeet or anyone scheduled for this afternoon, did they? Not after what happened."

She hesitated just a few seconds too long. Noel stiffened, and he felt his heart grow icy cold.

"No," she said quietly, "no one else has gone through the portal."

He jerked away and stood up, turning around to face her. "Did everyone come back?" he asked, his voice unsteady. He gripped her by the arms and shook her. "Are they okay?"

She said nothing. She didn't have to. Her face gave it all away.

He shoved her aside and stumbled forward, already running before he reached the door.

Intensive care lay at the rear of the infirmary. Seldom used, it now had the small medical staff bustling quietly in and out. A huddle of technicians stood outside, whispering and comparing data.

Noel hurtled through them, heedless of what they said or the hands that tried to snag him.

"Noel, wait!"

"Kedran, you can't—"

"Just a moment!"

He fought them off, too angry and scared to care what he did, and plunged through the ICU doors.

Inside, he stopped, his heart hammering at the muted wash of light over the beds, the monitors beeping softly, steadily, the medics glancing up to stare at him without expression. He gulped, his head going suddenly light as though it wanted to float far above the rest of his body. His knees had gone to water, but he refused to let them sag beneath him.

Not Trojan, he thought, letting the pain and grief fill him. Not his hairy giant of a pal, his best friend, the man he'd give his arm for.

The door to the unit opened behind him, letting in a slice of stronger light. One of the doctors raised his hand, and whoever entered behind Noel stopped. In silence they all watched while he pulled himself together and walked to the first bed.

Talia Baker lay there, her petite face drawn with pain, her skin so gray and lackluster she didn't look human at all. Her eyes were closed, and monitor clips were stuck to her temples, chest, and arm. Noel looked at the readouts and sucked in his breath. He didn't understand all of them, but what he did comprehend looked bad. Talia had been a traveler for sixteen months. She was the youngest, the newest of their number. This had been her third or fourth assignment. It looked like it would be her last.

Gordon lay in the next bed. Tall, blond, gentle—he was more scholar than man of action. He was on complete life support. The brain activity line registered nothing at all. Noel's eyes stung. He wanted to do something, say something, but there was nothing to do or say, nothing at all. Gordon was a dead man. If they turned everything off, he would lie there as still as the grave, never to make his quiet jokes again at the cafeteria, never to stay awake through Dr. Rugle's boring briefings again, never to walk up in his diffident way and ask a question about LOC function. His specialty had been mid-twentieth century and the Second World War. He had come back from travels with bullet holes in his uniform but otherwise unscratched and unruffled, always smiling, his soft, singsong voice unique among the others.

Now there was no Gordon, nothing but this shell of him breathing artificial air, dead blood pumping through a dead body, caught and crushed in who knew what kind of hell as the time stream failed around him.

Noel blinked back tears and realized he was gripping the bar at the foot of Gordon's bed, gripping it so hard his knuckles were white and his hands aching. He felt locked there. He couldn't move, couldn't make his head turn, couldn't force his feet to step to the next bed, and yet somehow he found himself at Trojan's side. His fingers closed around Trojan's cold ones. He steeled his jaw, but his mouth quivered at the emotions he could not hold back. His friend . . . he had lost his friend . . .

Someone touched his shoulder, and a voice said quietly, "He isn't dead, Noel. He's stabilized, holding his own. There's a chance . . ."

It took a while for the words to register inside Noel's brain. Finally he wrenched his gaze from Trojan's still, slack face and looked into the eyes of the doctor. "What?"

"I'm afraid he's in a coma. There's no telling how long its duration will be. Being the last to step into the time stream this morning, he was the farthest away from the whiplash effect of the distortion. It caught him last, after most of the force had dissipated. We have strong hopes of saving him."

Noel's gaze wandered back to Trojan. Trojan was the lucky one; the big, hairy one who always emerged unscathed from trouble. He pretended to be careless, yet he was organized, methodical, neat, and prepared. He claimed to work at the Institute strictly for fun. He was independently wealthy and had become a historian as a hobby, yet no one on staff was more diligent. He looked like a barbarian with his red beard, unruly long hair, and burly shoulders, yet he held several degrees from prominent universities. He was all the things Noel would never be, and now he lay here, far away and unreachable.

Noel drew in a ragged breath and stepped back. As long as he lived, he would never forget the haunting sight of Trojan lying there with the support machines around him, helpless and hurt.

Outside, the infirmary lights seemed too bright. The technicians surrounded Noel, battering him with questions. He ignored them all and walked to the coffee machine on feet he could not feel. The liquid was hot and bitter. He hated coffee, but he drank it fast, burning his tongue, wondering how Trojan could crave the stuff. It felt hot and oily in his stomach. For a moment as he crumpled the cup in his hands, he wondered if he would vomit it up.

"Everyone, please," said a clear voice, a voice that made him cringe, as though it flicked along a raw nerve. "Let Mr. Kedran have some space. Please. He'll answer your questions later, but now isn't the time."

Standing with his back to the room, Noel heard them shuffle out, still muttering to each other about equations and formulas and physics far beyond his comprehension. But the person who sent them away remained.

Noel bottled his rage and turned slowly to face the psychiatrist—a sleek, middle-aged Englishman. "Dr. Filingby," he said in as neutral a tone as he could manage.

"Noel," said Filingby with a nod. "Some unpleasant things have happened, haven't they? Why don't we step along to my office?"

Noel stiffened and tried to hide it. He had to hide everything, had to fool those brown, observant eyes. "I have another appointment. Could I drop by, say, in an hour or so?"

As soon as he spoke he knew he'd done it wrong. He'd been as sleek and civil as Filingby, something he never was.

The psychiatrist shook his head. "I know this has been a great shock. We're all very sad about Mr. Heitz and the others. You and I should sort this out immediately before the technicians come at you again. Don't you agree?"

"Dr. Rugle sent you."

Filingby's brows shot up. "Hardly. I came as soon as I learned you'd regained consciousness."

"You put me out," said Noel in sudden realization. "You sedated me."

Filingby made a deprecating gesture. "I know you hate it, but really you were in a bit of a state, rolling and screaming on the floor."

"I could have warned them. I could have told them what to do, but you knocked me out," said Noel furiously, unable to hold back the accusations.

"Nonsense. Neither of us could have helped these people. They were already caught in the distortion. By the time any of us knew what was happening, it was already too late for them. You can't blame yourself, Noel. You can't blame anyone."

Noel looked down, his eyes hot, his mouth grim. He knew exactly who to blame. Leon was behind this. Leon, who had remained in the seventeenth century. They could say all they liked about Leon not actually existing back there, but Noel knew better. What he had said to Dr. Rugle about his separation from Leon pulling the time stream apart had been right. He knew that now. He also knew there was only one thing he could do to stop the situation from getting worse.

"Now, Noel, don't be stubborn about this. It will help to talk through this. It really will. Let's go to my office for a few minutes."

"I'd rather talk to Bruthe," said Noel.

"Yes, well, the senior travel technician has his hands full at the moment, trying to keep the portal closed."

That startled Noel from his anger. "What?"

"Er, they're having a bit of a problem down there. Nothing they can't handle, of course, but—"

"Damn!"

Noel pushed past him and ran from the infirmary, ignoring

Filingby's shouts to come back. The lift balked after one floor, and refused to operate.

"Access denied," intoned an automated voice.

He jabbed the open button and stepped off. Jogging down the corridor, he passed rooms of technicians huddled over computers, their voices overlapping and shrill.

Someone looked up as he hurried past. "Hey! You can't go down there."

Noel was already ducking through the emergency stair doors. He scooted down the steps, only to pause on the landing as his knees went funny on him. If he hadn't been holding on to the railing he would have pitched forward into the stairwell. He clung there, gasping for breath, and wondered why the walls seemed to be pulsing around him.

Dismay filled him. Not another distortion.

But it didn't happen, at least not with the suddenness of the previous two. This was something different, something that made prickly sensations crawl across his scalp. His teeth started itching. His mouth felt as dry as powder. Every time he blinked, his eyeballs seemed to jolt loose in their sockets. And all through him he could feel, or sense, a mighty humming noise on a pitch too low for his ears to register. Rather, his bones seemed to pick it up, this humming vibration that seemed larger than the building, or even the world.

The time portal, he guessed with a fresh spurt of fear. It was open full tilt, and it was running out of control.

Below him, a door opened, and a figure in a shielded protection suit stepped into the stairwell. It gestured at him. "Go back!" it said, the voice muffled by the helmet. "Go back! You're making it worse."

Noel believed him without any conscious attempt to reason through it. He tried to go up the stairs, but his legs still refused to support him. He was reduced to crawling, dragging his lower body like a cripple. And each time he reached for the next step he was afraid his hand would go right through the solid matter.

The suited figure waddled up to him and gripped him by the arm. Pulling him upright, it supported him the last few steps, then pushed him through the door. He went staggering across the full width of the corridor and thudded into the wall.

The suited figure followed him, closing the stairwell door

and activating shielding and full lockout. NO ACCESS flashed above the door, and the weird sensations in Noel abruptly stopped. He sagged against the wall, breathing hard, but able to feel strength returning to his legs. The dizziness vanished, although he could still—faintly—feel the humming going on below in Lab 14.

Bruthe pulled off his helmet and glared at Noel. "Just what were you trying to do, wreck everything? We're barely holding containment right now as it is."

"How could I make it worse?" retorted Noel, but he had an idea—an impossible idea floating in the back of his skull— but one that went right along with his separation-from-Leon theory.

"Now what do you think, you and your reversible wave pattern?" said Bruthe with exasperation.

"I knew it," said Noel. "I knew it was Leon. We should have come back together."

"Apparently. I don't have time for that right now. Communications are shot, and I've got to give these readings to the secondary computers up here. Once we get the Time Computer closed down and the portal shut, we can deal with solutions."

"Bruthe, I—"

"Stand aside, Kedran. We've got a hell of a mess to deal with right now."

"I want to help!" Noel called after him in frustration.

"You aren't trained to deal with this," said Bruthe over his shoulder as he hurried away. "Just stay out of the way."

Noel pushed himself after Bruthe. "Wait," he said. "Talk to me."

Bruthe never slowed down. His heavy jaw was locked in a harsh line. "I don't have time."

Noel caught up with him and matched his pace. "Leon and I are two parts of a whole, right?"

"Hmmph."

"Our patterns are the same, aren't they?"

"No, they're like a zipper."

"Reversed."

"Of course reversed," said Bruthe, glaring at him as though he were mentally defective. "How else would you fit together?"

"And if we're not together, then the time stream can't function the way it's supposed to."

"You're getting delusions of grandeur, Kedran."

Noel cursed to himself and caught Bruthe's sleeve. "*Listen* to me. Our separation is an anomaly, right?"

"It's sure the hell something."

"And an anomaly in the time stream can theoretically cause distortions, right?"

"Yeah."

"So if I go back, then that should—"

Bruthe came to an abrupt halt and flung his arm across Noel to stop him. "Hold it. Where did you get that idea?"

"How else does it work out?"

Bruthe rolled his eyes. "The eggheads could tap out a whole series of combinations and possibilities."

"I'm not talking about an abstract problem," said Noel urgently. "I'm talking about myself. I know what's wrong. Look, I felt a distortion yesterday that didn't register. It happened to me, and no one else. I'll bet you my year's paycheck that today the distortion happened here because today *I* was here. Nature is trying to pull us back together, only we can't be put back together as long as I'm in one time stream and Leon is in another."

Bruthe stared at him a long while. "You're telling me you want to go back?"

"Hell no, I don't want to go back. But I have to. What happens if two time streams come together—and I don't mean just opening one a tiny bit for a traveler to slip through. I mean, really coming together."

Bruthe stared at him. "You know. Poof." He gestured with his hands.

"And how close are we to that . . . poof?" asked Noel.

"You know that too."

"So are you going to listen to me and *help* me, or are you going to go watch the eggheads run numbers through the computers?"

Bruthe stood there in silence a long while, so long Noel almost gave up.

"Bruthe!"

"Okay," said the technician reluctantly. "God knows, this is crazy, really crazy. You've got no rational basis for this, no formula."

"I've got my instincts," said Noel. "I *know* I'm right."

"You better be," said Bruthe. "Or it's over for all of us."

Noel swallowed hard, trying to ignore the nervousness that crawled up his spine, trying not to look ahead at what he intended to do.

Bruthe tilted his head. "Let's go run some numbers and set up a field of entry."

"You take care of that," said Noel. "I'm going to get a LOC."

"Arnie will program that. We'll need several—"

"No!" said Noel sharply. "Just you and me. I'll do the programming."

"You don't know how."

"I used to hang out with Tchielskov, remember? I can do it, close enough anyway."

Bruthe gasped. "Kedran, you're out of your mind! This has to be exact."

"We've got a Time Computer running out of control and you intend to be exact?" sneered Noel. "Speed is a little more important than—"

"No way! You want to get there with two heads? You want to come back with all your body parts reassembled in the wrong places? What do you think this is, mumbo-jumbo? My God, we're lucky we got Heitz and the others back in the right combination. This isn't a fly-by-the-seat-of-your-pants operation. It—"

"We have to hurry," said Noel with all the urgency he could muster. "We have to do it ourselves, and we have to do it fast." He held up his hands, which were shaking uncontrollably. "Another distortion is coming, Bruthe. I swear to you that I know. Rugle will stop us if you let her, and she'll be wrong. We have to act now while we still can."

Bruthe gripped him by the arms and shook him. "And I'm trying to tell you that I'm not sure we can get you back, not if you go in like this. Without prep or—"

"I have to take the risk," said Noel, everything in his eyes. If he couldn't convince Bruthe, then there was no chance at all. "I *have* to."

Bruthe's dark eyes met his own, troubled and filled with doubt. "God help you," he said at last, and turned back with him. "Let's go."

CHAPTER 4

∞

The protective suit gave him anonymity among the technicians rushing about the laboratories, except he had to move slowly while they ran and shoved in an effort to get their jobs done. Noel had never been claustrophobic, but the suit was stifling. He could feel sweat trickling down his back. Every breath inside the helmet was a clammy one. The suit had a fairly decent ventilation/air circulation system, but his nervousness kept him short winded and drenched.

Heavy shielding built into it enabled him to enter the laboratory area, but the vibrations humming through him were almost unbearable and every fluctuation in the wave patterns had his heart jumping in response. He could feel the relentless tug of the time stream. The open portal was like a maw, sucking at him with a greediness that was frightening.

Always before, he'd entered Lab 14 with anticipation and excitement. The portal had been a doorway into adventure and knowledge. Entering the time stream was a gentle experience, like walking through a dark mist to the other side.

But not now.

He walked in and stared at the portal, mesmerized by the pulsing, swirling violence on the other side. The gray void now resembled roiling storm clouds. A sharp flash of energy made the lights in the lab flicker ominously. Monitors shrilled and flashed screen after rapid screen of data. Warning lights sig-naled across the board. Inside the helmet, Noel's hair stood on end as though he'd received an electrical charge. Fear engulfed him. He couldn't step into *that*.

A technician bumped into him, almost knocking him off balance. "Hurry," said Bruthe over the helmet mike. "Take your LOC and a blank one from the safe, and then get out of here."

Ignoring him, Noel continued to stare at the portal, feeling it reaching for him, wanting him. It was as though the time stream had become alive, had taken on an intelligence. His rational mind knew that was nonsense. What he felt was simply the phenomenon of his wave pattern responding to those within the stream, but the superstitious, primitive part of him came clawing up out of control, pushing him to run from this place, to run and abandon everything in an effort to save himself.

Bruthe thumped his helmet to get his attention. "Noel! Take the LOCs and get out of here! Even in the suit, you're upsetting the slight balance we're able to maintain."

Noel nodded, trying to pull himself together. He turned his body slowly about, finding it almost impossible to move. His joints seemed to be glued in place, and the itching in his teeth grew worse. He could feel prickly, unwholesome things crawl-ing over his body and digging into his skin. It was just his nerve endings going insane, he told himself. Just nerve endings.

He fumbled at the safe, his gloved fingers unbearably clum-sy. His concentration grew fuzzy; his vision blurred. He knew he could not stay in here much longer. He knew also the danger if he went mad and threw himself into the time stream with neither LOC nor destination. His hands were shaking so bad he had to enter the security code four times before he hit the proper sequence.

The safe opened, and inside it the LOCs were all activat-ed—flashing green, blue, pink, or any of the other colors in the normal spectrum, each according to its isomorphic code. They shouldn't be on, not in here, but nothing was work-ing right.

He grabbed his, the blue light flashing across the pale gray surface of his suit. He selected one of the blanks flashing white. Withdrawing his arm, he started to hit the closure control, then on impulse seized Trojan's LOC as well.

The loudspeaker blared over the general noise: "Noel Kedran, report to Dr. Rugle's office immediately. Noel Kedran, report to Dr. Rugle's office immediately."

Noel closed the safe with a snort of defiance. If the hag thought he was going to sit by meekly while her analysts asked him questions and the whole place went up in smoke, she could think again.

He shoved the LOCs into his pocket and blundered from the lab on stiff, shaking legs. In the corridor, it was better. He sagged against the wall with a sigh of relief, then jumped as a warning klaxon sounded.

"All personnel move to safety stations. All personnel move to safety stations."

Alarm rose through Noel. Another distortion must be coming, right now. And he wasn't ready. Pressing his arm across his pocket, he started running slowly, clumsily, his legs as responsive as lead. He'd taken only a few steps when the warning klaxon failed in mid-shrill, and the lights went out.

Plunged into absolute darkness, Noel lost his balance and fell. *Not again*, he thought in despair, but when he went down he hit the floor immediately. His outflung hand struck the wall, which was standing upright and normal, just where it was supposed to be. A distortion wasn't happening.

"What the hell?" he said aloud.

The lights flickered, then went out and stayed out. The Institute had powered down.

At the far end of the corridor he heard noises, footsteps, low voices. Hand torches shot beams of light here and there. Still lying on the floor, Noel realized belatedly that the vibration was gone. The crawling, itching sensations were gone. His joints had unlocked, and he could move freely again. He sat up and tugged off his helmet, feeling hollow with astonishment and dismay. The time portal must be closed.

"Kedran?" called Bruthe's voice. "You out here? Kedran?"

A hand torch came closer, brighter. It shone in Noel's face, making him squint. He shielded his eyes. Behind the light he could make out Bruthe's blocky shape.

"Kedran?" said the technician. "You okay?"

"Yeah," Noel said, and staggered to his feet. He felt lost, the adrenaline in his veins streaking without purpose now. After pumping himself to be a hero, to face his own secret fears and overcome them, it was over before he could do anything. Strangely enough, he felt let down, almost disappointed, and a little angry about it. "She pulled the plug. Dr. Rugle pulled the plug."

"She had us cut the main generator power to the Time Computer and portal," said Bruthe heavily. His voice dragged with fatigue. "It's down. It's all down and finished."

Something in his tone caught Noel's attention. He opened his pocket and fished out his LOC. It was no longer activated. The circuitry lights had stopped flashing. Pulling off his glove, he held it clenched in his bare hand until the LOC grew warm from his touch.

"LOC," he said. "Activate."

Nothing happened.

"The Time Computer's down," said Bruthe gently. "LOCs can't run without it. Nothing runs without it."

"Yeah, well, when we power up again—"

As Noel spoke, the main corridor lights flickered and came on, making him squint. Bruthe switched off his hand torch. Down the corridor, there was scattered applause and a few cheers. Bruthe glared at them. "Fools. They'll really clap when they find they're out of a job."

"What do you mean?" asked Noel. "Bruthe, what's the matter?"

"Guess."

Noel stared at him a long time. Then his eyes widened and he sucked in a quick breath. "Oh, no . . ."

"Oh, yes. We had hold of the time stream the way a boy holds the string of a kite. We turned it loose. We let it go. There'll be no getting it back again."

Noel frowned, trying to comprehend what he was saying. "The past is gone? We can't go there again?"

"No more travel," said Bruthe heavily. "No more recordings. No more research."

"But originally, years ago, when the time stream was discovered and accessed, that was based on—"

"It was a fluke. The only thing those experiments and long years of research did was to make a little jiggle, and we accessed the time stream by accident. The old boys were smart enough to grab on, and they built a whole science on top of that lucky break."

Bruthe threw up his hands. "There you are. In all the years I've worked here, old Rugle has been so cautious she made a glacier look like a speedway. Then, under the first by-God truly cosmic-serious crisis we've ever had, she makes the one and only gut-instinct decision in her whole life, full speed ahead, and damn the consequences."

Bruthe's voice dripped with bitterness. "I guess I could be unkind and say the old broad lost her head and panicked. Maybe under the circumstances it was understandable. It certainly worked."

"It can't be closed off forever," said Noel, refusing to accept Bruthe's pessimism. "You'll figure out a way to—"

"Kedran, you live in a dreamworld of romance and happily ever after. You're so used to flitting back to the days of yore when all things were possible that you can't cope with a little hard-core reality."

"But the technology remains, Bruthe!"

"And we don't understand it anymore!" Bruthe shouted back. He met Noel's astonished gaze and turned red. "Back when the Institute was founded, they had some pretty sharp scientists working way out there on the far reaches of inverse quantum physics. I have the data, the notes on file, sure, but I can't follow what they were doing. Arnie can't. Meissen takes stabs now and then, but she really doesn't understand much more than we do. Old Tchielskov might have, since he worked with some of the early people, but he's dead. It's over, Noel. You'd better start polishing your résumé for a new line of work."

Tossing his gloves and the hand torch into his helmet and clapping it beneath his arm, Bruthe marched away.

Slowly the Institute started on mop-up procedures. Rumors spread quickly, demoralizing everyone from the data clerks on up to the travelers and administrators. When officials, including the owners of Work Complex 7 and representatives from the mayor's office, showed up and were conducted to Dr. Rugle's office, talk circulated around the place again.

Noel avoided the clusters of people talking in the halls. Shedding his protection suit, he went to the infirmary to check on Trojan. The reception area was blocked with a crowd of people suffering cuts and other minor injuries. Someone was crying in hysteria. The medical team had its hands full filling out forms and asking questions. One nurse laden with scanning equipment was making routine checks for radiation poisoning, although for what reason Noel couldn't determine. The Institute wasn't nuclear fueled, and the time stream carried no radiation within it.

Noel backed away and circled around through the narrow service hall, where medical deliveries were made and where the medics came and went. Only staff were supposed to use this entrance, but no one was checking security. Noel slipped in through the doctors' lounge—empty—and went straight to intensive care.

The beds in ICU, however, were empty.

Noel stood there stricken, holding Trojan's LOC and looking about as though if he stared hard enough the patients would rematerialize.

"Trojan?" he said, feeling a lump growing in his throat. "Trojan?"

"Hush," said a nurse, appearing behind him without warning.

Noel jumped as though he'd been shot and turned on her. "Where are they?"

"You aren't supposed to be in here," she said severely. "No visitors—"

"Where *are* they?"

"Where are who? We have our hands full right now treating more cases than we're equipped for and . . . how did you get in here anyway?"

"The travelers who were brought in earlier today. Baker and . . . and Heitz. Where are they?"

The nurse's expression turned grim. "Are you a technician? How did you get in here? You aren't allowed in here. No one is."

As she spoke, she started toward him. Noel held up his hands in a placating gesture, but his mouth was set with stubbornness. She wasn't going to toss him out until he had a straight answer.

"Trojan is my friend. The last time I saw him he was strapped to this bed, right here, and was on support machines. If he's dead, I want to know about it!"

"Noel," said Dr. Ellis's soft voice. "Don't shout, please."

Noel turned, startled again. He frowned into her face, anxious, seeking answers. "Why the games, Doc? Where is he? What's going on around here?"

She sighed and took his arm. "That will be all, Nurse."

"Yes, Doctor." Disapprovingly, the nurse left.

Noel felt cold, and he didn't like the way she was beating around the bush. "Come on. Tell me."

"I'm sorry. I'm not trying to spread out the suspense," she said quietly. "Trojan regained consciousness when the power was cut off."

Delight spread through Noel. "He did?"

"Yes, he—"

"Then he's okay? God, you really had me worried there. Where is he?"

"Noel, please listen to me," she said, cutting him off. "He's been transferred to . . . another unit."

"What? Where? Transferred where?"

"He was quite unmanageable when he awoke. Incoherent, raving, violent."

Noel blinked, not understanding her. "Trojan? No way."

"He was hysterical, screaming. We had to sedate him heavily, I'm afraid. One of the medics, Dr. Reingold, was injured in the struggle to subdue him." She pushed back her blond hair and showed him where a bruise was beginning to darken her temple.

Frowning, Noel turned Trojan's LOC over and over in his hands and thought about it. "You're telling me he's gone to the rubber room."

She sighed with annoyance. "The psychiatric treatment center is designed to *help* travelers. Slapping bigoted labels on it undermines its purpose."

Noel looked down, one corner of his mouth jerking, but he didn't make an apology. He was too angry to retract his words. "Its purpose *is* bigoted. Who got the idea in the first place that going back in time would make us crazy? It hasn't. The stress is minimal—"

"*Your* experiences weren't exactly pleasant," she said.

He stopped, expelling a breath, and glared past her at the wall. "No," he said curtly. "They weren't. But that doesn't justify Filingby and his goons—"

"At the moment Trojan Heitz is exhibiting signs of acute

dementia. He is disoriented, confused, and we cannot make contact with him."

"You mean he's—"

"Yes, Noel. I'm sorry. At present, he's quite mad."

Noel clenched his fists at his sides. "Because of the distortion. Because of being jerked back through it like that."

"Yes."

Noel scowled at the floor, his jaw working. His eyes stung and he had to wrench his head up to look at her. "His chances?"

"It's too soon to tell," she said. "He's very strong and healthy, physically. Talia Baker died when the power was cut off. Our auxiliary systems cut in seconds later, but she was holding on by such a fragile thread, she couldn't . . ."

Dr. Ellis's eyes filled with tears and she swung away from him. "Damn! I hate losing patients. I hate losing them to unseen causes. There were no physical injuries to these people. Whatever they saw, whatever they experienced in that time stream was so dreadful, so horrible, their minds could not cope with it."

She swung around to face him. "You're the only one who knows what it's like when it goes wrong. You're the only one who's gone through anything approximating that and survived."

In spite of himself, Noel flinched. "I can't—"

"Noel, you've got to cooperate with Dr. Filingby and talk about it. For your friend's sake, if not your own."

He shook his head, feeling the protests boiling inside him, knowing that she wouldn't understand his refusal, knowing they were going to get angry at him all over again. But how could he make them understand that talking about it, describing it, meant reliving the nightmares in his waking hours as well as in his sleep? He'd tried facing it on his own, and it hadn't helped. He'd tried facing it in a few sessions with Filingby, and it had made things worse.

"For Trojan's sake," she repeated. "You say he's your best friend. Do you really care about him? Do you, Noel?"

Noel held out the LOC to her. "Let him wear this, okay?"

She took the LOC from him, and her mouth pursed with emotions she wasn't going to express. Tears glimmered briefly in her eyes, but she held them back. "It won't help him now," she said quietly.

"It won't hurt him," said Noel. He refused to meet her eyes.

She sighed. "Go and talk to Filingby," she said. "The slightest detail might help them figure out what to do."

Noel said nothing. She had him boxed, and they both knew it. Only what Trojan needed wasn't going to come from shrink sessions or tests. What Trojan needed had to be fixed in the past, somehow. And the past had been shut off from reach.

CHAPTER 5

∞

"Noel," whispered the voice through deep layers of sleep. It was a dark, gravelly voice—rough, as though from smoke and whiskey—a voice that reached through the eddies of dreams and subconscious fragments. "Wake up, my brother. Wake up."

Noel stirred unwillingly. His body was dead tired; his eyelids had been glued shut with sleep.

"Noel," whispered the voice, so familiar. "Wake up. I know how to help your friend. Listen to me."

He dragged opened his eyes and sat up before his mind was entirely alert. "Leon," he said clearly.

The sound of his own voice woke him up. With a blink he looked around the conference room, and saw faces staring at him from around the table, saw the litter of coffee cups and electronic notepads, saw Dr. Rugle glaring at him from behind the lectern.

"Mr. Kedran," she said icily, "you have snored through two-thirds of this meeting. Unless you have finally thought of something worthwhile to contribute, please do not interrupt the proceedings."

The heat of embarrassment flared in his face. He felt like a schoolboy caught by the teacher. The others cast him glances of sympathy, consternation, or impatience. From the looks of things, Rugle was still justifying her decision to power-down the portal and still refusing to let them try to activate it again.

"I'm sorry, Mr. Bruthe," she was saying now, while the senior technician glowered at her. "The safety of the Institute must override all other factors. We cannot possibly make any attempts to reactivate the Time Computer until we understand exactly what caused the problem."

"But our work, our research," sputtered one of the scientists.

"Delays are regretted but unavoidable. Until we have a firm basis to—"

Noel scraped back his chair and stood up.

She glared at him, then assumed an exaggerated expression of patience. "Yes, Mr. Kedran?"

"I think we've all got a very clear grasp of what's behind the distortions," he said.

She scowled. "Wild theory will not—"

"Hold it a moment," he said, putting up his hand. "I don't have to express myself in technical terms to be understood at this table. A few months ago, you people performed a manual return, broke the time loop where I was trapped, and pulled me back. But you didn't get *all* of me."

"Mr. Kedran—"

"Just shut up," he said.

Her mouth flew open in astonishment, but before she could speak, he continued, "I know you looked at the wave pattern and determined it was too slight to cause much trouble. I accepted that at the time because I didn't want to see my duplicate again. In fact, I was happy to leave him behind me."

"Go on, Kedran," said Meissen, her thin face keen with interest.

"Well, it's like a grain of sand that gets inside a clam shell. One grain of sand that irritates the soft lining of the tissue there."

"Yes, yes, and a pearl results," snapped Rugle. "What is the point?"

"The point is that Leon has irritated the fabric of time. However slight he is, his existence remains a problem. We know the time stream is delicate. We've always been careful to slip in and out for short periods, never too greedy, never trying too much. Our motto has always been no disruptions."

"Exactly!" said Rugle. "And now we must leave things alone until they stabilize."

"Hiding your head under the carpet isn't going to make the problem go away," said Noel angrily.

"We have contained the—"

"No, ma'am, you shut the door. That's something else entirely."

"What do you mean?" asked Meissen.

"He means," interjected Bruthe, thumping the table with his fist, "that if Leon is causing the time distortions, they will continue whether we have access to the time stream or not. And if those distortions can no longer reach into our century, then they will—"

"Affect a different century," finished Meissen for him.

"I was afraid of that," said Wemble, a third, extremely elderly technician. "Treating the symptom and not the cause."

"Foolish."

"Thought so at the time."

"Should have moved more slowly."

"Hasty judgment and ill thought out."

"No thought at all."

"I had the whole series of calculations running for a steady down-sizing of the situation. We were this close to control."

"Please!" said Rugle, red cheeked. She rapped the table. "Out of order. Out of order."

"To hell with order," said Noel, glaring at her. "We can sit in meetings and waste hours, or we can do something to clean up this mess."

"I will not authorize any attempts to power-up the portal!" shouted Rugle. "That is my final word. If you cannot or will not agree to finish this meeting in an orderly, productive fashion, then I will exercise my prerogative to call an adjournment."

Bruthe turned to Meissen. "I still don't think we can regain access, even if we bring the Time Computer on-line."

"It's worth a try, though," she said. "Erskine is going through the archives now to look up the original procedures. If we can integrate those with—"

"I see," said Rugle furiously. She started scooping up papers and her notepad. "Very well. Persist in discussing it among yourselves as a theoretical exercise. However, I will not authorize any activity in Laboratory 14 *or* Laboratory 12 until we've had time to cool down and examine this in a rational light. This meeting is adjourned."

She swept out, pausing only to glare at Noel. "You will report to my office immediately, Mr. Kedran. Immediately."

He stood there, his hands jammed in his pockets, and said nothing. As soon as the door closed behind her, he turned to the others.

"What do you think? Can we try? I know Bruthe has his doubts, but—"

"If we got the portal open again," said Meissen slowly, her brow knit, "what exactly would you do with it?"

"Return to 1697, where I last parted from Noel, and—"

"You mean Leon," said Bruthe.

"Yes, Leon," said Noel impatiently. "Of course Leon."

"You said Noel."

"What?"

"You said Noel."

"Oh, leave him alone, Bruthe," said Meissen with a shake of her head. "It was just a slip of the tongue."

"Go on," said Wemble to Noel, who had found himself unexpectedly flustered by the slip. "Return to Leon and do what?"

"Bring him back with me," said Noel. He pulled the blank LOC from his pocket. "Give him this. Program it to interact with mine, and then use it for retrieval."

"Simultaneous retrieval," said Meissen thoughtfully, her eyes alight with mental calculations. "Rebonding in the time stream."

"A reversal of the original duplication process, you mean," said Wemble.

"*If* we could make it work," said Bruthe, gloomy with doubt.

"We have everything from the archives," said Meissen impatiently. "I don't see why we can't."

Bruthe snorted. "I meant the rebonding process in the time stream. It's a dubious objective."

"A pretty problem," said Wemble, his quavery voice shaking with excitement, his rheumy eyes glowing. "But let me see . . . yes, we have the LOC that was sabotaged. We know exactly what Tchielskov, poor fellow, did to it. We know how the time loop was closed around you, Mr. Kedran. Yes, a pretty problem indeed."

He sat back in his chair, mumbling to himself, his thoughts miles from the rest of them.

Meissen smiled at him. "He'll come up with a theory for us to try. That is . . ." She hesitated, gazing up at Noel, who was still standing. "If you're willing to go back in."

One of the other scientists, who until now had sat in silence, leaned forward. "Seems to me there are a great many ifs, very large ones."

"Oh, who asked you, Speratkin?" said Meissen with a flip of her hair. "You're on Rugle's side. I'm surprised you didn't leave with her."

"You're all talking big here," said Speratkin, "but without authority from Rugle there's no trying any of this."

"And if we do it," said Meissen, her eyes flashing, "can Rugle stop us?"

Speratkin smiled derisively, but his gaze went to Noel. "You are leading a mutiny, it seems."

"Oh, hush," said Meissen. "It's not a mutiny. We aren't rallying around one traveler. It's a question of solving a problem scientifically. Kedran's right about us closing the door on it and hoping it will go away. I'm concerned about the exponential effect of that distortion bulge being shifted into some other century. There's no telling which way it could go . . . into the past perhaps or possibly our future."

"And there is another problem you are not considering," said Speratkin.

"By all means, point out yet another problem," said Bruthe darkly.

Speratkin pointed at Noel. "Him."

"What? Why?" asked Meissen.

"He's unstable. He's not certified to travel. How do you know he could even handle returning through the time stream, especially as rough as it is now?"

Noel scowled, telling himself to keep his temper. Speratkin had a point, however sharp.

"I'm not certain anyone could survive travel under the present conditions. We lost three today. Three! Casualties like that have never happened before—"

"You lost two," said Noel.

Speratkin's gaze never wavered. "Three. Heitz is insane. If he recovers—"

"When he recovers—"

"Face facts, Kedran. I realize he was a friend of yours, but—"

"I'm sure the medics are doing all they can," put in Meissen hastily. She shot Noel a warning look and shook her head.

He held back the argument on the tip of his tongue. "I know I'm not certified, but that's part of the—"

"Bruthe!" said Speratkin. "You're senior travel technician. Can't you explain to this fool that we can't guarantee sending him in one piece, much less bringing him back?"

"I explained it," said Bruthe.

"Yes, and now you want to try something fancy while he's spinning around in the void? I think you are all indulging yourself in flights of pure fancy. It cannot be done."

"And so we shouldn't try?" said Meissen scornfully. "Is that it? Just sit here, the way Rugle wants us to, and do *nothing*?"

"The anomaly could fade," said Speratkin.

Noel snorted.

"Yes? And why not?" persisted Speratkin. "It is only recently that the problem has grown worse. If we plotted it, I am sure we would see a bell curve of increasing disturbance until the distortions themselves became large enough to register. There is every chance that they will fade away just as they came. You do not want to overreact. There has been, surely, enough of that today."

No one said anything.

Noel glared at Speratkin. He'd been close to getting them fired up enough to try, and this pet of Rugle's had to ruin everything. Noel felt a fresh burst of temper, then shivered as though the adrenaline drained from him all at once. He couldn't get angry, couldn't let them see the rage and frustration eating holes in him. He had to get out of here before he started yelling and made enemies of them all.

Shoving his hands back into his pockets and clenching his fists there, he swept them all with a look and said, "Well, think it over. I've got to . . ."

Letting his voice trail off without realizing it, he left the room in a rush.

Outside, he felt a tremendous sense of relief, as though oppression had been lifted from his shoulders. Not bothering to analyze that, he wiped the sweat from his face and stopped, staring at his hand.

It was shaking.

He curled his fingers into a fist, afraid it was happening again and not knowing what to do about it.

How could a distortion reach him now with the portal closed? Impossible. Yet . . .

He stood in the corridor, not daring to move, not certain he could. The lights seemed dim, and he wondered if the power was being affected. He didn't hear an alarm. In fact, he didn't hear much of anything.

The silence had closed around him stealthily, without him noticing it, until all the sounds faded. He tried to swallow away the dryness in his throat, but he couldn't. He thought he should move over to the wall, but he couldn't take a step. He was frozen in place.

The corridor ahead of him swelled into a bulge, the walls curling into it, widening around him. He stiffened, frightened of the effect. A terrible coldness swept over him, a coldness that sank so deeply and instantly through his body it was like death.

Behind him the conference door opened, and the technicians filed out, gesturing and talking among themselves. He could see their mouths moving, but sound remained cut off. There was only the dimming light, the bulging walls, the silence, and the numbing cold.

They would see him. They would sound the alarm. They were coming right toward him. They would help him as soon as they noticed. They had to notice. They had to see that something was very wrong.

But they walked right by him as though he did not exist. Bruthe was speaking to Meissen, who smiled and shook her head. She glanced back at Wemble, who was shuffling along in a daze, his thoughts still a thousand miles away.

"Help me!" called Noel, except no sound came from his throat.

They walked away from him, scattering, some vanishing through the curve of the walls and disappearing, others fading into the shadows.

"No!" cried Noel. "Come back!"

But no one could hear him.

Desperation gripped him. Was he fading too, dissolving somehow through the distortion into the time stream itself? Without a destination, without his LOC linked into the Time Computer, he would be lost forever, sucked into a void without end, to spend eternity nowhere.

Wasn't that what had happened to Leon? asked a tiny voice in the back of his brain.

I'm not Leon! he raged, struggling to break free of whatever paralysis held him. *I don't deserve his fate!*

A flash of color seared his eyes. He blinked, squinting against it, then flinched as more color passed by him, almost on top of him.

For a moment he was surrounded by shapes and colors, all abstract and incomprehensible. He squinted, trying to look at them, trying to understand, and after a moment he thought he began to recognize a circle, large and turning.

No, it had spokes . . . it was a wheel. Circles and squares meant a wagon. Flashes of color, large and too fast to capture. He concentrated, struggling to make sense of it. People, perhaps?

Sound came then, babbling layers of it, rising and falling in volume, scaring him with unexpected shrieks that pierced his hearing, then murmured lower, all of it going too fast for him to catch any particular words or phrases, even to be certain it was language at all.

And he smelled something pungent and unpleasant. He smelled pigs.

With that single recognition came a sense of triumph, filling him for the space of a heartbeat, before he comprehended something else. It was the sound of a pig grunting, low and unmistakable amid the cacaphony of noise. A broad blur of crimson swooped at him and sailed over his head, making him flinch.

He squinted, listening to the pig, trying to find it with his blurred vision that was so out of sync with this world. From the sound of it, the animal must be rooting right at his feet. But he couldn't see it, couldn't feel it. He could only smell the strong barnyard stench of it, and then, for an instant so fleeting he might have imagined it, his outstretched fingers felt something firm. Flesh, hair, warmth. He had touched the pig.

Everything went black, and he felt himself hurled backward.

Then he hit something solid, and crashed through it with a deafening noise. He was still falling, through splintering, cracking resistance. There was light and commotion around him, the smell of dust, and pain.

Something heavy landed across him, and he heard someone shouting for help. Noel opened his eyes and found himself lying on his back with bits of wall and board on top of him. Puzzled, he tried to figure it out. Had he materialized in a wall or just fallen through one? And where was he now?

A face appeared over his. Soft blond hair brushed his cheek. "Noel? Noel, can you hear me?"

It was Dr. Ellis, the peach who kept him at a professional distance no matter how often he tried to close in. Noel blinked and sneezed, sending plaster dust flying around his face.

"Doc," he gasped.

He tried to raise his head, but she held him down. "Just lie still a moment. Your foot is still caught in the wall. They'll soon have you free."

He raised his head anyway, but couldn't see anything for people crowding around. "What? My foot? I don't—"

"Stand back," said Dr. Ellis. "Give him some room. I want a gurney here right away."

He gripped her wrist. "No shots. Promise me!"

The tremors in his hand were violent enough to shake her arm. She frowned and put her other hand on top of his. "Okay. No shots right now. But promise me you'll remain calm."

He drew in a deep breath, afraid of the tremors, but knowing he could hold himself together. He would do anything to avoid being sedated and made helpless.

Another medic joined Dr. Ellis. She said, "His body surface temperature is very low. Scan him and make sure you record everything, no matter how peculiar. Let's wrap him in the thermals and see if we can't thaw him out."

She had to pry his fingers off her wrist. They swathed him in blankets and lifted him onto a self-powered gurney. By now Noel realized he was in one of the data centers. Terminals and desks were all around him. The workers stood in a huddle, talking among themselves and looking frightened. There was a man-sized hole in the partition wall. He could see right through it to the corridor outside.

But it wasn't the same corridor, or even the same floor he'd been on when the distortion had caught him. Noel tried to sit up.

"I . . . I c-can walk," he said, stumbling over the words. "I'm b-better."

"Why don't you just take a little ride with us," said Dr. Ellis smoothly, keeping her hand on his chest as they guided him down to the infirmary. "You're still a bit unsteady. Let's not rush anything."

Dr. Rugle, her craggy face creased with worry, stood at the infirmary doors when they arrived. "Doctor, I want details on every—"

"Yes, of course," said Ellis, brushing past her. "But not right now. We've got hypothermia and shock to treat."

Noel chuckled to himself, glad to leave the old bat behind. By the time he realized they had stripped off his clothes and were wrapping him in a very strange material, he found Dr. Ellis had vanished.

"Doc!" he shouted, gripping the sides of the shallow bath they were trying to immerse him in. "Not c-cold. C-cold pigs in there b-but no found m-me."

"Please," said a nurse, struggling with him. "Just relax. This solution will raise your body temperature. It will help you feel much better."

"P-pigs!" he shouted, frowning as he realized he wasn't making sense. They pried his grip off the edge of the bath and got him into the warm solution. But the cold didn't leave his bones, and the shaking didn't stop. He wanted to tell them they were treating the wrong symptoms, but he couldn't get his tongue to link properly with his thoughts.

Dr. Ellis reappeared, her pretty face creased with a frown. "Noel, you're not responding the way I'd like. We need you to settle down."

"No shots!" he gasped out, and was pleased that made sense. He struggled to raise his hand, fighting the wrappings they had on him. The tremors racked his body, and he couldn't stop his teeth from chattering. "No sleep n-now. N-need Bruthe here."

"Perhaps later, when you're stabilized."

"*Now!*" he said with all the force he could muster. He glared up at her, infuriated by his helplessness. "No t-time for l-later."

She reached behind her. "Noel, I'm sorry, but I can't keep my promise if you don't keep yours."

"D-don't put me out!" he gasped, desperate to make her understand. "Won't help."

"Yes, it will. It will relax you and give you some rest. Your body needs—"

The syringe came at him, but he managed to knock it from her grasp.

"Noel!" she said in annoyance. "You mustn't—"

"Listen!" he said. "M-must listen to m-me. T-tell Bruthe."

"All right. I'll give him your message," she said. "But then you must rest."

He shook his head, but realized he couldn't waste time arguing with her when she so plainly did not understand.

"Going again," he said, concentrating on making himself as plain as possible.

"What do you mean?"

"*Going.*"

"Another distortion?"

He nodded, then found he couldn't stop his head from bobbing. He shivered, racked with a new chill so pervasive his heart almost stopped.

"Dr. Ellis," said a voice, breaking in. "His symptoms correspond to traveling without preparation."

"What?"

"Yes, it's very odd, but that's what the bio-comps say."

"*Going,*" said Noel. "Going again. Went this time."

"But the portal is closed."

He winced. "Doesn't m-matter. G-got to p-protect m-me until . . ."

He struggled, unable to continue.

She reached into the bath solution and took his hand. Her grip was reassuring. "Until what?" she asked.

"Until Bruthe is . . . ready," he said. "T-tell him I went. Saw a . . . a . . ."

"Yes? What did you see?"

"Saw p-pig. There b-but not in sync. He'll understand."

"So do I," she said grimly. "But with the time portal closed, how—"

"G-got to hurry. P-program LOCs. Wemble hurry." He gasped for breath, closing his eyes in exhaustion. The shivers wracked him constantly now, sapping his strength. It would come soon. This time, he might not return. "T-taking me, ready or n-not."

"Doctor, his readings are fluctuating wildly."

"I hear you," said Dr. Ellis. "Prepare another sedative."

Noel lacked the strength to protest. He lay there, eyes half-shut, unable to stop the little moans that burst from him, feeling his heart skip and race. Travel sickness, they called it among themselves as a joke. He'd never had it before; he had always been so thoroughly prepped because of the precautions and safety measures Rugle insisted on that he'd sailed through travel easily. Once in a while there was a little nausea, and he always arrived ravenously hungry, but that was minor. This was god-awful, worse even than his sabotaged plunge through the time stream when Leon had been created and he'd thought he was going to die in the void.

And he was scared, scared down to the little dark corners of his soul, because nothing had kept this effect from reaching him. If the shut portal was no barrier, then what safety did he have?

Sooner or later, ready or not, he was going into the past.

CHAPTER 6

∞

Curled inside the bubble of protective shielding like a chick inside its egg . . . faces and voices coming and going, fragments of comprehension laced between spans of madness when the time stream reached for him and only the thin barrier of technology kept him safe.

"Noel, we've managed to unravel some of the equations. There's a chance of getting the portal opened and back under control. Of course we'll have to wait until a distortion occurs before we can try to activate. It's risky . . ."

"Noel, your LOC has been reprogrammed. The parameters are very clearly defined. There'll be no problems this time."

"Noel, as soon as you find Leon, you will have three days in your time to get this LOC on him. As soon as you do, he'll be recalled. That will trigger your recall sequence, and we'll be able to bring you both back at the same instant. That is . . . if we have the Time Computer fully operable by then. It's only fifty-two minutes, more or less, on our side to get it right."

Noel lay at the bottom of the bubble, curled up against the constant shivering and sporadic cramps of pain. He listened to their voices but could not always answer. They were all working hard on his behalf and it troubled him that he could not express his gratitude. More and more he seemed to be in a dream, as though he had been implanted with head chips. It was a foggy place where reality and other time slipped side by side, interchanging without warning, one or the other becoming incomprehensible or clear at any given moment. He understood now what had driven Trojan insane. This was the madness, this being caught between times, unable to *be* in either place. They had brought Trojan's body back through the distortion, but his mind still lay trapped. Did they understand? They were prepping Noel to return to his last point of travel. Would they return Trojan to his last visit coordinates as well?

"Noel, time for more conditioning," said Dr. Ellis's voice. "These are subcutaneous implants. Your translator receiver and immunizations. They'll hurt a little."

The burning sensation in his forearm was far away. Noel turned his head, trying to look at her.

"I know. I'm sorry," she said, her voice warm with care and sympathy. "It won't hurt long."

"Send Trojan back," he said, focusing all his will on those three vital words. "Send . . . him *back*."

She patted his shoulder and closed the bubble. "Rest a while now. They'll be ready soon."

He frowned, curling himself up tighter. Had she heard him? Had he even managed to speak aloud? He had to make them understand.

"Ellis," he whispered. "Ellis!"

But the babble of incomprehensible sound, the ghostly voices and shrieks of things not understood, gnawed upon the fringes of his mind. He lay still, refusing to surrender to the flash of shapes and color that were all of the wrong size and perspective, too fast, too frightening to follow.

The lid of the bubble opened, letting in a rush of lab-scented air. Blinking against the dazzling light, Noel struggled up, damp and dazed like something newborn.

They lifted him out and garbed him in breeches, coat, and buckled shoes with tall heels. His LOC was fastened to his left wrist. Leon's LOC was fastened to his right. They gave him a sword and a pistol and a plumed tricorn hat.

"There's a packet of food in your pocket for when you arrive," said someone. "Eat it all immediately. It's high carb and packed with special nutrients to get you over any exhaustive side effects of travel."

The old man had a familiar face, but Noel could put no

name to him. He looked around at the others, and could not remember their names, either.

"You think he's getting this?" asked the gloomy, dark-faced man. He was unshaven, and his eyes were red rimmed with fatigue. They all looked tired.

The blond woman came to Noel. Her face was like an angel's; her spun-gold hair gleamed under the lights. She ran a scanner over him, peered closely into his eyes, and gave her head a slight shake. "I can't tell. His brain wave patterns have altered too much. They're getting closer and closer to Heitz's all the time."

"Then we're doing all this for nothing. Risking the equipment, risking our careers by going against Rugle's orders, for *nothing*."

Their talk went on, circling Noel, but he stopped listening to it. Tremors shook in his hands. He lifted them, curling and uncurling his fingers, aware in some dim periphery of his brain that there was significance to this particular discomfort.

"He's shaking," said the woman.

"Right. It's coming then. Open the portal."

The words themselves had no meaning, yet something in Noel understood. He sat upright on the table and turned to face the metal doors now spiraling open. Beyond them . . . beyond them should have been a gray mist, a wonder undescribable.

But there was nothing. Just darkness, empty and unremarkable.

Noel stared at it, blinking slowly, the unnatural cold creeping by relentless degrees through his body.

"Powering up . . . computer coming on-line."

Around the lab, lights flashed on as boards powered to life. Digital readouts came on in sequence, and the staff hurried to initiate systems checks.

"Can we catch it? Can we grab onto it?"

"Don't know yet," said the grim-faced technician, his fingers going like lightning over the controls. "God help us if we do catch it. I'm not sure just what we'll have."

The woman stood at his shoulder, glancing back only once at Noel. Her face was pale with concern. "And the time destination?"

"Final programming going in now," he replied absently, his fingers working the keypad. "London, England . . . 1697. Got that. Now for the specific month and day . . ."

"Can you find Leon's wave pattern?" asked the woman anxiously. "Can you pinpoint it?"

"No . . . it's scattered worse than it's ever been. None of these readings look right. Look at how they're fluctuating back and forth. They should be steady."

"If we boost?"

"No! It won't work. Too dangerous to send him like this. We'll have to abort."

"But, Bruthe—"

"I said *abort*! Close it down."

Even as the technician reached for the controls, the distortion came. The walls rippled and shuddered. One moment Noel's surroundings looked normal; the next they became bizarre and incomprehensible. The shapes that had once been equipment, tables, and chairs bulged and mutated into abstractions. Then they shattered into fragments that went spinning around him. Light came, so blinding his eyes watered and squinted, and he could hear a thundering roar.

He wasn't sure how long the disorientation lasted, but at some point the light dimmed by steady degrees, becoming less blinding, then tolerable. It coalesced into a ribbon of sparkling light that coiled in a tight spiral, then unfurled across the lab with unbelievable speed. The curls in its length snapped taut and arrow straight as it came toward him.

Fear drew him up. He faced it, mesmerized, his heart hammering wildly in his chest. He knew instinctively that it was aiming itself directly at him, that it *wanted* him. In that instant his fear battled with curiosity. This was something new, something never before witnessed by mankind. Nature always sought to bring aberrations back into line with her laws. He and Leon had created such an aberration, and time itself was reaching for him now.

His pulse hammered. His breath felt locked inside his chest as though his lungs had turned to stone. In his life he'd been able to face most crises with courage, but before this onrush of raw cosmic energy, his fear grew overwhelming. He turned to run.

The ribbon of light pierced his back like a spearhead, its violence so unexpected, so *sharp*, he could not find enough breath to cry out. Impaled on it, lifted by it, he felt the radiance surge through him, filling him. He flung up his arms, his back arching against the force of this energy man was never designed to experience. It seared through his body with a coldness like fire, and he thought he would explode from the pressure of it inside him. Just when he could stand it no more, it burst from his chest and careened to the far side of the lab. Now he was threaded on the stream of light like a bead. Twist and struggle though he might, he could not pull free.

Catching his breath at last, he screamed.

The sound issuing from his throat was absorbed into the energy band. The fiery stream continued flowing through his body while the front tip of the light ribbon swept up and down, probing the far corners of the lab. Still suspended on it, being lifted or dropped as it undulated and coiled, Noel held out his arms and saw himself bathed in an eerie backwash of colored light. His skin had taken on a radiance of its own, lit by the energy flowing through him. Sparks danced from his finger-tips, and a blazing corona surrounded his head. His hair blew back from his face, and he could feel his skin hardening into something brittle, like a carapace.

Across the lab, the open portal filled with a strange, unearthly luminescence. Within it, ripples of multiple energy bands crossed and sparked. The plasmic maw began to swirl, to roil with gathering force, feeding on the distortion itself yet supplying it in turn as a loop was generated.

With a mighty crack of sound that could have shattered the world, the tip of the light ribbon found the open portal and speared through it, clearing a pathway through the heaving, swirling mass of cloud and energy vapor. For an instant Noel saw to the other side with unexpected clarity. The shapes there were no longer peculiar and frightening. They were now in sync with his own dimension. They matched his reference concepts of reality. They became comprehensible for the first time. He saw people jostling along a muddy street. There were horse-drawn wagons, pigs rooting in the sewage, and vendors crying their wares. He smelled the stench of unwashed humanity, garbage, and animals. Their voices and clamor reached him like a beam of hot sunlight.

"Noel?"

Hearing that cry, uttered *here* on this side of the portal, he managed to turn his head. Dr. Ellis was on her feet, her hair standing on end from the electrical discharges in the room. He saw the others—Wemble and Bruthe, Meissen and Arnie, Pitsdon-Wells and even Speratkin—all crouching for cover behind tables. Their faces were seared with colors man was not meant to experience. Their eyes shone with fear and wonder.

He held out his hands, still streaming with the energy that coursed through him. "Send Trojan back!" he shouted with all his might. "He's out of sync with time. He must go back. Do you hear me?"

"I hear you," said Dr. Ellis. "But, Noel, you can't—"

Lightning forked from the portal into the lab, jabbing raw energy into walls and setting circuitry on fire. Black smoke boiled over the pungent stench of burning optics. The street scene within the time portal vanished behind a curtain of smoke. Everything in the lab stopped still, even the energy stopped coursing through the ribbon. Noel felt as though he had been suspended on a frozen conduit. He found himself holding his breath, waiting . . . waiting for what?

The distortion began to recede, and the energy wave reversed itself.

Still speared upon it, he screamed again as the light ribbon was drawn backward through him. The smoke-wreathed walls rippled and twisted. Tables teetered and fell over as though the entire building were being shaken. Noel expected the energy wave to vanish, thus letting him fall to the ground. Instead he found himself moving with it, passing through solid objects without feeling them, flying straight for the swirling, roiling, horrifying mass of energy just beyond the open portal.

Fresh fear swept him, blotting out everything except the horror that he faced. Not like this. He didn't want to go like this.

He forgot what lay at stake. He didn't want to enter this wild time stream. It was engulfing him, absorbing him, killing him.

Pain sheeted him in waves, a pain so encompassing he could not endure it. Yet there was no blacking out, no means of escape. The LOCs on his wrists activated and grew hot, burning into his flesh. His skin, so thickened and hardened only moments before, now seemed to melt and run off his bones, the pool of it separating into individual globules that floated past his face. Images flashed through his brain too rapidly to comprehend; a blurred collage of faces, voices, and memories screamed past him.

He was becoming a different entity, transforming from matter to energy, changing from an object to a streak of light, leaving one dimension for another.

Then, with a mighty boom of sound, he was sucked through the portal into absolute, terrifying darkness, spinning around and around without reference point. The energy wave inside him vanished, leaving him drained and empty. He was nowhere, no*when*. He was nothing.

In that moment he went mad.

Lost, he fell into the darkness, sucked down and down into the vortex of no return, a place of no existence, the void between dimensions. Screaming without voice, his mind was driven to the stark edge by the terror of it.

From somewhere in that nothingness, there came Leon's face, *his* face, laughing at him with wild lunacy. The glee, the satisfaction, the gloating all emanated from Leon. Noel understood. They were trapped here together, chained to the perpetual hell of nonexistence. For Leon it was the ultimate joke; for him it was the end.

The last cohesive part of him cracked and began to crumble. He could not hang on, could not hold himself together.

Then, like a lifeline, he heard Tchielskov's soft, precise voice: "Remember this, my boy. When you travel, you are stepping off the cliff of reality into the void of eternity. You must create your own reference points. None will exist there save those you provide for yourself.

"Think of where you are going. Find one clear image and cling to it with all the mental power you possess."

For no reason at all, Noel thought of the pig. That huge, hot, smelly beast rooting in the muddy street.

He stopped spinning in the darkness. Like an arrow shot from a bow, he went hurtling through an ether that lightened into grayness, then into silver, then into a pale radiance, then into sunlight hot and fiery.

Spat from the time stream back into reality, Noel went tumbling head over heels through a mud puddle and smacked into a rickety fence made of woven sticks. He lay there a moment, winded and dazed. The ground was hard beneath his cheek.

Damp mud soaked through his clothing. He felt sunshine burn into his back like an iron. The earth stank. The air stank. He coughed and dragged in a breath with difficulty. His lungs struggled as though they hadn't operated in a long while. It was hard to believe that he'd survived his passage through the time stream, much less actually come out safely on the other side. And yet, here he was on solid ground.

Fuzziness clouded his mind. Something nudged his side, then nudged him again with more force. Noel tried to focus.

Survival. He was somewhere, in the past. Actually there, here, somewhere sent, without friends, had to move, had to live, had to find . . . had to find . . .

Leon.

Noel's mind cleared so abruptly it was like a slap. For the first time in weeks he felt whole, freed from the uneasiness that had plagued him since his separation from Leon. His energy and optimism came bouncing back. Just getting here had been a tremendous achievement. And although he did not want to think about facing the time stream again, he knew that he could—he *would*—find Leon and restore the rip in the time fabric that their separation had caused.

He rolled over on his back, ready to sit up. But over him loomed something large and furry. It snuffled his ear and grunted. He found himself looking straight into the ugly snout of the largest sow he had ever seen.

Tiny piggy eyes stared back at him. She snorted, her large snout working. Her mouth chewed something, and he glimpsed wicked teeth.

With a gasp, he jerked out from under her, scrambling up to his feet with a stagger and turning around to find himself in a small pen holding several more swine.

A stick whistled through the air and crashed down upon his shoulders. The blow nearly knocked him flat. " 'Ere, ye thief," screeched a voice like a rusty hinge. "Bold as brass ye are. What're ye doin' in my pigpen?"

Whirling around, Noel ducked in time to avoid another blow. He found himself confronting a wizened old woman, her gray straggling hair bound back with a bright kerchief, her body shawled and gowned in rags, her stockinged feet kept above the mud in tall pattens, and a pipe stuck in the corner of her toothless mouth.

Her eyes blazed with fury, and she swung the stick at him again. "Get out o' there, ye thief. Blackguard! Knave! Ye'll no steal my shoats."

The pigpen, as rickety and transitory looking as it was, stood at the corner of a wide juncture in the street. Apparently this was a meat market of sorts, for nearby was a pen full of honking geese, and beyond it hens fussed and cackled. On the other side, a boy in grimy rags guarded a basket of fish that looked none too fresh in the withering heat.

Numerous merchants and customers stood about in clusters. They haggled for prices, pinched merchandise, and shook their heads, but when the old woman started shouting and hitting Noel with her stick, they all gathered around to watch and laugh. The men were for the most part bearded and long haired, standing in doublets and baggy breeches. Dust coated their wide-topped boots. The women, white faced and tall on pattens to clear their long skirts of the dust and dung, wore broad, rather shapeless bodices that hung from their throats to their hips, then wide skirts, all layered and gathered down to their feet. The unflattering garb made most of them look fat. Faces powdered white with lead and rouged, their hair knotted and frizzed into a profusion of ringlets, they were garish and unfriendly, and their voices shrieked over the general din.

"Tear into 'im, old woman!"

"Ooh, isn't 'e a strapping one? Fair makes me 'eart flutter."

"With mud all over 'im? Pah!"

"I likes 'em like that, dark and dangerous," said another, winking at Noel.

Distracted, he neglected to duck in time, and the old woman's stick thudded into his back with enough force to make him yelp.

"That's enough!" he yelled at her.

"Enough, is it?" she shouted back. "I'll show ye enough, ye dirty—"

She swung wildly at him, but he dodged that one. In doing so, however, he tripped over his sword and fell to one knee. Mud splashed around him. The crowd roared with laughter.

"Well, now, Dame Grace," said one fellow, his voice booming over the noise. "Is that any way to treat a customer?"

"Customer?" shrieked the pig woman, taking another swing

at Noel, who scrambled out of the way. "Witch, more like! I seen 'im come right out o' the thin air itself. 'E's a familiar, workin' fer Old Scratch!"

Several people drew back with gasps, and some made furtive warding gestures, or crossed themselves. Noel, aware that this could get ugly fast, jumped to his feet and called out, "I'm nothing of the kind. All I want is a proper young pig for dinner, and this is how I'm treated."

"Hah!" yelled the old woman. "Where's 'is money, if 'e's a customer? Where's 'is servant, come forth to 'aggle fer 'im? Impostor! Scoundrel! Devil!"

Wound up again, and swinging the stick with every accusation, she chased Noel around the pen once more, sending disgruntled pigs trotting from one side to the other.

There was no point in talking to her, no point in making up an explanation. Calling attention to himself was not what a traveler was supposed to do. His job was to blend in and remain unobtrusive. It was, Noel told himself, time for a strategic retreat.

Ducking from the rain of blows that came down relentlessly upon his head and shoulders, Noel tried to leap the fence but caught his toe and came tumbling down. The fence fell with him, and with squeals the pigs bolted into the laughing crowd.

"Ham tonight, mates!" yelled someone, and the race was on after the fleeing animals.

"My pigs! My livelihood! Ye thief! Ye devil! I'll 'ave yer 'ide nailed to my wall fer this," she cried, beating him with more force than before. "Magistrate! Guards! 'Elp!"

Noel rolled beyond her reach, dodged a hand that reached for his coattails, and darted into the crowd as fast as his legs would carry him.

"Catch the blighter!" yelled someone.

"Catch the witch!"

A pair of women standing directly in Noel's way shrank from him, screaming hysterically.

Muttering curses under his breath, Noel veered around them and picked up speed. A man came at him, but Noel thrust him off and ran down the street.

Behind him, he could hear the pig woman screeching and other women screaming, one claiming his touch had burned her arm. Their stupid superstitions annoyed him, especially since he knew they could whip themselves into a mob frenzy with very little trouble. He had no desire to be the target of a witch-hunt, and he ran as fast as he could with one hand on his sword hilt and the other on his hat. Within a few yards, his legs began to burn and stagger. His breath came in harsh wheezes, and his heart was bursting.

He knew he could not keep up this pace long, yet a glance back told him his pursuers were still coming.

"Seize that man!" yelled one. "That man running! Aye, the one in the blue coat. Seize him!"

An individual with a badly pocked face attempted to grab Noel's sleeve. With a snarl, Noel shoved him aside and veered down another street that was narrower and choked with pedestrians.

He could not run in this crowd, and it was wise to slow down and call less attention to himself. Whipping off his hat, Noel tucked it beneath his arm and did his best to blend in among the thick of them.

Glancing back, he saw his knot of pursuers had dwindled and fallen behind. But they were still coming. He saw one spot him and point.

"There he is!"

"Damn!"

Cursing, Noel whipped between two mule-drawn carts laden with apples and turnips, saw an alley, and ducked into it.

At once, his gut shrank with dismay. Alley or street, it was narrow and dark, barely wide enough for two men to walk abreast, and it stank of raw sewage.

It had the look of a trap, yet he dared not return to the larger street. His strength was draining fast from the exertion. A stitch went through his side. The ravenous hunger that was a travel side effect gnawed deep within him, taking his resources too fast.

Dashing up a set of rickety steps, he flung himself into a doorway, panting hard and shrinking back into its recesses as much as possible.

The men plunged by the mouth of the alley a moment later, pausing to peer into it, arguing among themselves, then running on. Noel closed his eyes a moment in relief and stayed there a few seconds longer to catch his breath.

He was nearly faint with hunger and burning with thirst. Something to drink was not available, but he pulled out the food packet and devoured its contents greedily.

He knew he was taking a risk by staying here. The men might double back, and if they did he'd be in real trouble. But the food revived him a bit, and he remained in the doorway until he'd gobbled every last crumb.

By then he had his wind back, but his legs were still trembly and cramping with fatigue. Concerned, Noel massaged his calf muscles. He was lean and fit. During the past few weeks of his hiatus at the Institute, he had worked out daily to keep himself in shape. Running this distance shouldn't have taxed him at all, but he felt as though he'd gone a marathon.

Maybe his wild ride through the time stream had sapped him more than he knew.

Taking no chances, he opted not to return to the busy street but instead continued up the alleyway, thankful to have ditched his pursuers so easily.

It was a gloomy hole he'd wandered into, however, and the farther he progressed the worse it looked. The walls on either side grew even more narrow until his shoulders almost brushed them. The mud he sloshed through had an appalling stink, and he dared not examine it closely. A rat as large as his foot darted across his path. The creature paused at the sight of him and stared up, its red eyes unafraid and malevolent. Noel halted, seized by an instinctive revulsion, and waited until the rat scuttled out of sight through a hole. Noel could hear the squeaking of other rats from inside the house foundations.

No people were about. He might have been the only person alive in this quarter. The quiet was spooky, almost unnatural after the thronging crowd in the other streets.

His stomach was already growling with fresh hunger. That wasn't normal. The food packet was high in energy and nutrients. It should have lasted hours, but he felt as though he hadn't eaten anything. His legs were cramping again, harder now, the pain making him sweat.

But Noel hurried on, the hair on the back of his neck prickling. He didn't like this place with its quiet, its dark gloominess, its filth. Some of the houses had strange symbols marked on the doorways.

Crooked and winding, the street went on as though forever.

The houses loomed overhead, seeming to lean on their ancient timbers until they nearly touched.

Laundry, half-soured and unable to dry where the sunlight didn't reach, hung on lines suspended from upper-story windows. The foundations of the wooden houses were green and peeling with mildew. An air of rotted dampness permeated the place. He would have paid a king's ransom for a breeze, but the air lay still and hot and fetid.

A cat fight erupted beneath a doorstep, and Noel's heart jumped into his throat. He thought about turning back, but being arrested for pig thievery or witchcraft didn't appeal to him. He stuffed his hands deep into his coat pockets and kept going.

Finally he began to encounter signs of human habitation. Babies wailed from indoors. Voices cursed or laughed or argued without care for who overheard.

"Gardyloo!" cried a voice from an overhead window. Seconds later, a stream of liquid splashed down, missing Noel by scant inches.

He jumped back, swearing, and glanced up. The woman, her hair hidden inside a large mobcap, waved at him with a cheeky grin and pulled her chamber pot back inside.

"Too bad I missed, ducks!" she called saucily. "Ye look like ye need a bath."

"Not the kind you're offering!" he called back.

"Oho!" she retorted with a toss of her head. "Too good to be doused in 'is Lordship's piss, are ye? Might make a man o' ye."

"Might not," said Noel, and went on his way, grinning.

After his exchange with the chambermaid, the street seemed less sinister. A few minutes later he emerged onto a larger road. The buildings stood well back, and the sunlight made him squint beneath his hat brim.

This was a heavily traveled thoroughfare, one a-bustle with foot, horse, and carriage traffic. A coach horn blared tinnily, making him nearly jump from his skin. Pedestrians scurried aside for a coach and four driven at a furious pace. Dust fogged up in a cloud that settled over everything.

Coughing and slapping his clothes, Noel walked on. He tried to look for a street sign, but found none. He had lost all sense of direction, except what the sun's position told him.

It was afternoon, growing late. No one seemed headed home, however. If anything, the crowd grew thicker.

Noel was obliged to push his way past vendors carrying trays of pastries or delivering buckets of water to houses. Coach horns blared impatiently to force a way for the men and women in finery of silks and lace being borne along in carriages, their liveried guards riding with them for protection. The coachmen swore vividly and cracked their whips over people and horses alike.

He saw cutthroats surveying the crowd, urchins picking pockets, beggars whining and holding out their bowls for alms. Now and then he encountered elderly or middle-aged men in plain, Puritan garb marching along with frowning, disdainful faces. These types, with their black coats, long-pointed white collars, and unadorned headgear, stood out in marked contrast to the more colorful clothing everyone else wore. Buffoons sometimes followed these Puritans, making faces and rolling their eyes to the laughter of the passersby. There were inns flowing with custom, their doorways thronged with laughing cavaliers in tall riding boots and extravagant plumes flowing from their cocked hats. They made bets among themselves or laughed over women's scented handkerchiefs that they passed around. Children flirted with danger as they darted across the street in front of horses, and starved dogs stole scraps from the gutter.

Noel kept one hand on his money purse, the other on his sword, immeasurably comforted by the pistol in his pocket and searching for a safe place where he could consult his LOC for a self-check. By now, especially after eating, he should have been revived and alert. Instead, he still felt shaken. His hunger increased with every step, and his body ached with a strange exhaustion.

Maybe Dr. Ellis hadn't managed to condition him properly for his passage through the time stream. But, no, she wouldn't neglect a single detail. The woman knew her job.

On the other hand, that hadn't exactly been a normal travel. No one could have foreseen the events that had transpired in Lab 14, least of all Noel. He was simply grateful he'd arrived in one piece.

He had three days in which to find Leon in this teeming mass of humanity, but he was optimistic. All he had to do was activate his LOC, and it would find Leon for him.

The somber thumping of a drum carried over the noise, growing steadily louder. People stopped in mid-conversation. Their faces grew pale, their expressions taut. A general uneasiness flashed over the crowd. Curious to see what was coming, Noel paused and glanced over his shoulder.

Like autumn leaves blown by a wind, pedestrians cleared the street. They pressed back against the storefronts and doorways, their fear an odd contrast to the general gaiety that had been present moments before.

"Death cart!" wailed a voice in an eerie parody of a vendor's cry. "Death cart! Make way."

The drum boomed steadily, and now Noel could see a thin, bewhiskered man walking in a long, loose coat that resembled a robe. His hat was pulled low over his eyes. He led a cart horse that plodded slowly with its head down. A child followed the cart, his expression like stone. He beat upon a drum with one great solemn thump after another.

"Death cart! Bring out yer dead. Make way fer the death cart."

The cart was piled with corpses sewn into crude shrouds or wrapped in blankets. One of the cart's wheels bounced over a pothole, and a blanket slipped back to reveal a woman's face, gray-white with death, her eyes open and staring, terrible pustules blemishing the corners of her mouth.

Watching, Noel felt the coldness of horror slide over him. At his side, a plump, elderly woman pulled her shawl over her head and began to weep.

"Plague victims," whispered Noel aloud.

"Bless us, dear Lord," murmured the weeping woman, clasping her hands together. "Deliver us from misfortune and protect us from the filthy air."

"It's not the air that causes bubonic plague," said Noel before he could stop himself. "It's—"

"Leave her be," said a man, giving Noel a shove. The woman turned and hurried away. "That be Dame Stoken, of Holborn. Lost four children to the plague last year, God bless their souls. It ben't so bad this summer, though it do be mortal hot now."

"Aye," said another fellow, talkative now that the cart had passed by. "Last year, we thought the end of the world had come upon us. Death carts was all the traffic there was, most times. And at night, mercy but how people did cry out and moan. Fair made your hair stand on end, it did. You never saw so many houses marked with the sign to keep away. Doctors dropping like flies, and you never knowing when the fellow next to you might break out with the fever. It got so a body was afraid to step out even to buy a meat pie for his supper.

"When the king moved his court to Oxford, why, I said to my wife, time we moved to the country too. And so we went. Just closed up shop and left it for anyone to take. But when we come back in the cooler weather, all was safe as houses, and waiting for us."

Nodding, Noel moved on. In his mind he was busy turning over this unwelcome information and trying to remember if 1697 had been a plague year. It seemed not, but this era wasn't his specialty.

Besides, he found other details that didn't add up. He was supposed to be in London, and the people spoke English, all right, but there was an odd look to the city, something unfamiliar and strange that he couldn't quite put his finger on. As he walked, the sense of something wrong grew stronger. Noel frowned and began to observe with greater attention details of customs, manners, and dress.

Sea gulls squawking amid the sparrows and pigeons told him this ramshackle city was a port, although he saw no ships or wharves. Hoping to establish his bearings and regain his sense of direction, he walked with the main press of the crowd, glad to see that the people around him were looking increasingly prosperous, and the area less seedy. As a historian, although not a specialist in English history, he was quite familiar with the famous landmarks of London. It was a handsome city, an old city filled with tradition and grand examples of fine architecture. Yet where were these mighty edifices? Where were the statues, the baroque park gates, the classic Wren-designed buildings of stone and brick? Too many buildings were built of wood. They looked old as well, almost medieval, although the people were clothed fairly similarly to what he wore.

Still . . . he eyed the men strolling by in wide-topped boots, their spurs jingling, swords swinging arrogantly from beneath their coattails. None of them wore a long vest like his. Their breeches were longer and fuller than his, positively baggy compared to his slim ones, and decked out with ribbons. He wore a tricorn, but their hats had straight crowns and large round brims. Many had either long hair or wore elaborately curled wigs down to their shoulders. Noel's own black hair was cropped short, and with the sun glaring from a hazy sky he was thankful not to be wearing a hot wig.

Granted, the last time he'd visited 1697 he'd been in the Caribbean among pirates rather than city dwellers, and fashion had hardly been important, but even so the men had tied their hair back, not worn it full and loose in this manner. Their clothing had looked more eighteenth century than this. The garb he saw now made him think of musketeers, cavaliers, and Louis XIV.

Noel swallowed hard, and a sudden qualm made him stop in his tracks. Someone bumped into him from behind, and he felt clumsy fingers nip under his coat. He grabbed the pickpocket's hand and dragged the boy around.

"Please, sir! No 'arm, sir. Please, sir."

Noel shoved the boy away and continued on at a fast stride, searching actively now for a place of privacy. His earlier sense of confidence had vanished, and he felt worried and shaken. He thought he'd landed in the right place—maybe—but certainly at the wrong time.

What had happened?

The semihysterical urge to laugh at that question rose up and choked in his throat. As though he needed to ask. Any of a thousand things could have gone wrong. All he had to do was remember his wild passage through the time stream. Bruthe hadn't had a constant fix on the destination. The distortion had been skewing all the data. He could be anywhere.

And if he'd landed in the wrong place or just the wrong time, then . . .

Gulping, Noel tugged his hat lower over his eyes and hurried on, threading a rapid path through pedestrians and riders, his heart thudding faster with every step.

Ahead, somewhat to his surprise and consternation, he saw the buildings end. The street narrowed to a country road. Meadows stretched over the hills, with small clusters of houses scattered here and there. He'd walked all the way to the edge of town.

To his left stood a posting house busy receiving carriages

and sending them off, the yard heavy with dust as hostlers hurried to harness up fresh horses and lead away the tired, sweaty ones to the stables around back. Smoke curled from the chimney, and Noel could smell meat roasting for dinner. His mouth watered, and his stomach growled hungrily. Men lounged around the doorway, holding tankards of ale, and he swallowed his own spit in acute thirst.

There would be time to go in and buy himself all the food and drink he wanted—later. First he had to access his LOC. He might as well find out the truth about where he'd landed and get it over with.

Noel hurried across the road, then paused at someone's well and helped himself to a ladle of water from a wooden pail sitting beside it. Refreshed by the drink, he slipped behind a garden wall, took a couple of apples from a heavily laden tree, and hurried out into the common meadow beyond.

A handful of sheep—their wool tangled with burrs and dried mud—stood listlessly some distance away. Noel looked around but saw no evidence of a shepherd. Still, the pasture itself was too exposed for his purposes. His shoes crunching on the drought-brittle grass, Noel took shelter behind a thicket of hawthorns and crouched there in the slice of shade they afforded.

Doffing his hat and balancing it on his knee, he ate one of the apples, core and all, then pulled up his left sleeve while he munched more slowly on the second piece of fruit.

His LOC, also known as a Light Operated Computer, was a complex marvel of miniaturized optic circuitry. Fitted with molecular shift in order to disguise itself to fit into any era, the LOC had changed itself this time into a braid of tawny human hair that encircled his wrist. It was tipped with gold at the ends in a clever kind of clasp. Noel raised his brows wryly. Passion's souvenir? Lovelocks? It was a bit too sentimental for his style. Who had programmed his LOC this time?

He took another bite of apple, feeling the inside of his mouth pucker at its greenness. He'd probably end up with a bellyache, although the fruit hadn't done much to alleviate his hunger.

In one of the houses several yards away, male voices rose in argument. Noel peered around the thicket of hawthorns with caution. In the distance, one of the sheep raised its head and looked as well.

Still all clear.

"LOC, activate," he said quietly.

The LOC shimmered, and the braid of hair was replaced by a clear-sided bracelet that flashed blue light. "Working," it replied.

Relief filled him. He realized that unconsciously he must have been expecting it to be damaged the way it had been during his last trip into the past. But it was in good order this time. He wasn't going to be trapped again.

Except you're in the wrong time, whispered a voice to him.

A chill ran down his spine that made the summer heat meaningless. He shook it off.

"Identify place and date," he said.

The LOC flashed. "London. August thirty-first, 1666."

Dismay sank through him. He frowned, refusing to believe it.

"There must be a mistake," he said. "Repeat command. Identify place and date."

"Affirmative. London. August thirty-first, 1666."

His frown deepened. "Repeat date."

"August thirty-first, 1666."

"Impossible. It's supposed to be 1697."

"Negative."

"Scan your diagnostic codes. Any—" His voice caught in spite of himself. "Any malfunctions?"

"Negative malfunctions. Date is August thirty-first, 1666."

"But that's thirty-one years off," he said, half to himself. "Why here? Why now? Dear God, why now?"

"I am not programmed for speculation," said the LOC tonelessly.

Noel remembered Bruthe saying something about Leon's pattern fluctuating. But even if the technician had failed to get a solid fix on Leon's whereabouts, theoretically he and Leon should have been drawn together by the time stream whether a mistake had been made or not.

A twist of scorn passed through him at his own thoughts. Someone had warned him against depending on theory. Besides, if Leon were around he should have turned up by now.

"Scan mode," Noel said sharply. "Is Leon in the city?"

"Unknown."

A small sigh, almost a moan, escaped him. He recognized the

hopelessness in his own voice and stiffened his spine immediately. There was no point in losing his head. He had to cope with this, and cope with it fast.

"We're in the wrong time," he said. "LOC, is recall possible?"

"Mission parameters have not been achieved," said the LOC.

"You mean, we haven't linked with Leon yet," he said, and rubbed his forehead.

"Affirmative."

"Are you programmed to scan for Leon's pattern?"

"Define Leon."

"Great," muttered Noel. "Didn't Wemble tell you what to look for?"

"Define—"

"Stop," said Noel. He paused a moment, feeling a tiny nerve twitch rapidly in his jaw. He had to stay calm. He had to believe that he wasn't trapped again. There was a way to overcome this . . . this small glitch. He had to remember that prep had been a little sketchy. The technicians had succeeded in getting him to the past. It was up to him to overcome the gaps.

But a thirty-one-year gap? How was he going to get around that?

He shoved the doubts away.

"Okay," he said aloud, expelling his breath. "I can do this. I can think my way through this. Of course. LOC, activate and link with Leon's LOC. It's programmed with Leon's pattern. Isolate and identify that, then scan for him."

He waited a moment for the spare LOC on his right wrist to activate, but nothing happened.

"Come on," he said impatiently. "I can't do it for you. The other LOC is programmed to work only for Leon. Tap into its internal codes and link—"

"Impossible," said his LOC.

"It can't be impossible," said Noel angrily. "That's the whole point of this trip. We have to find Leon and get this other LOC on him in order for—"

"Impossible."

He started to swear, then told himself it was just a machine. "Specify impossible."

"Impossible."

"Stop!" he said sharply. "Are you malfunctioning?"

"Negative."

"Thank God. Explain why you can't link with Leon's LOC. If you can't identify Leon as yet, then link with the LOC on my right wrist. You can scan that, can't you?"

"Negative."

"Why not?"

"Negative."

Alarmed, Noel pushed up his right sleeve. There was no bracelet of braided hair around his wrist, no bracelet of any kind. The other LOC wasn't there at all.

Disbelieving it, he felt of his arm. He pulled off his coat, swearing under his breath as he struggled with the garment. He detached the lace ruffles at his wrist and looked inside his sleeve in case the LOC had fallen off. But there was no spare LOC to be found.

"LOC," he said, his breath catching oddly in his throat. "Leon's LOC, is it anywhere on my person?"

"Negative."

"But it was. I mean, I did have it when I entered the time stream, didn't I? I couldn't have imagined that."

"Affirmative."

"Affirmative *what*? Did I have it when I entered the time stream?"

"Affirmative."

He was sweating. Almost absently he pulled his coat back on over his vest and linen shirt. His hands weren't steady. "Did I lose it in the time stream?"

"Other LOC detached in time stream . . . affirmative," said his LOC.

"Can you scan for it? Is it here, somewhere? Can you find it?" he asked.

"Negative."

"You can't find it?"

"Negative."

He tried very hard to keep his voice calm. "Would you mind elaborating on that response?"

"Specify."

"Damn you! Why can't you find it? You're a LOC. It's a LOC. If it's in this location and time, you ought to be able to pick up its energy wave. After all, the seventeenth century isn't exactly overrun with little computers."

The LOC flashed for a few seconds in silence, almost as a rebuke for his sarcasm. He knew he was projecting human reaction onto the machine, which was foolish, especially since it lacked artificial intelligence. Before he could say anything, however, it answered.

"Within parameters specified, discovery is possible. Leon's LOC is not activated. No energy wave can be detected."

Noel stopped gritting his teeth and thought about that for a moment. "But once it is activated?"

"Scanning possible."

"That's more like it."

But as swiftly as his spirits rose, they plummeted again. His LOC hadn't said the other computer had materialized here. It just said it was possible. The only individual who could activate it was Leon, and if Leon wasn't here, either, then . . .

He wasn't going to worry about it just yet. He had to have hope in . . .

What? Blind luck?

If he failed to find Leon, he would be recalled back to the twenty-sixth century, and the distortions would start all over again. He would end up completely insane.

Noel sighed and looked up into the lavender-hued sky. Twilight had cast long shadows across the meadow and pooled them where he was crouching. The air lay still and close. He got to his feet.

He couldn't search in the dark. He would get himself a room in the inn, some supper, and he would come up with a plan of action for tomorrow.

Somehow.

CHAPTER 7

∞

The Horse and Crown was a sprawling inn constructed of timbers, stone, and brick. Morning glories blooming white and blue ran along the thatched roof. An enormous thorny rosebush grew in a great arch above the doorway. The musky perfume of roses filled Noel's nostrils briefly before he ducked inside and was assaulted by the mingled odors of wood smoke, unwashed bodies, and ale.

The taproom was crammed with men of all classes clustered about the scarred wooden tables. Most of the customers had tankards in their fists. Numerous candles and the fire blazing on the hearth provided ruddy, uneven light. The windows were open to the evening air, but the room remained too hot for comfort. A pair of buxom serving girls hurried back and forth, their hair straggling about their flushed faces, their bare forearms as pale and firm as marble, their ample bosoms on display beneath a dewy mist of perspiration.

Somewhere, an ox was roasting.

The delicious smell of it almost made Noel swoon with anticipation. He found a place in the corner, keeping to the shadows away from the unnecessary fire, and took off his hat.

"Name yer drink, dearie," said the serving girl wearily. She had a round, kindly face and blue eyes. The man sitting next to Noel gave her rump an affectionate squeeze, and she swatted him off the way she would a pesky fly. "We got ale, port, and stout. Burgundy will cost you—"

"I'd like dinner, please," said Noel.

His request earned him a second look from her. She smiled. "Well, now, ain't yer manners nice. Dinner'll be cold mutton or a fine roast just finishing up this hour. We can serve the cold meat straightaway, but ye'll have to wait on the roast a bit."

"The mutton's fine," he said, ready to eat the table. "Anything, as long as it's quick."

"Peckish, are ye, sir?" She showed him a pair of dimples. "And to drink?"

"Ah . . ." He was afraid that as hungry as he was, any drink would send him skyrocketing. "Something mild—"

"Nothing like the home brewed," said his neighbor, smacking his lips.

"Ale," said Noel.

"Very good, sir. I'll bring it right across." She left with a swish of her generous hips.

The man next to Noel chuckled. "Fine sight, ain't she? Our Becky's a fine armful of a woman."

"Yes," said Noel, in no mood to become a drinking buddy to the man, who had a hooked nose adorned with warts, was missing most of his teeth, and hadn't bathed in days.

Across the room, at a long trestle table, a company of men in vibrant garb lifted their glasses in a toast, then burst out with laughter.

"Stranger here?" said the man at Noel's elbow.

"Um."

"Thought so. Thought at first you were one of the actors at yon table. Got that look about you."

Noel turned his head and looked at his companion, not certain how to take that remark.

The man grinned, displaying a few blackened stubs of teeth, and nudged Noel slyly in the ribs. "You know. The look of a gentleman and the speech of an educated man, without being either of those things."

Noel frowned, and the man raised his hands quickly.

"No offense to you, sir. I'm known for speaking plain." He smiled and laid his forefinger alongside his warty nose.

"Ah, you've traveled a long road down to London, now, haven't you?"

"You might say that."

"Looking all done in with the road dust coating your throat and a great gnawing hole in your belly."

Becky returned with a swish of her skirts and set a foaming tankard in front of Noel. She set one in front of the other man as well and gave him a sharp look.

"Now, Robert Mallory, none of yer sly ways tonight. There's a hanging at Tyburn tomorrow. Let that be a lesson to ye." She flashed her dimples at Noel. "The mutton'll be out directly."

He took a cautious sip of the ale, and found it surprisingly good.

Mallory clapped him on the shoulder. "Drink hearty! I told you it was good. Becky'll keep your cup filled all night."

Noel shifted to the far edge of his seat, trying to get upwind of the fellow. "One will do."

"What are you? A Puritan? Your pockets are flush. Why worry?"

A tiny alarm rang in Noel's head. "What makes you think I've got money?"

Mallory grinned evilly and leaned so close his rank breath wafted into Noel's face. "Why, sir, you ordered without asking the cost. A man who's well before the world is a man who doesn't care about prices."

Noel kept his expression neutral, but inside he was spinning with questions. What kind of man was he sitting next to? A pickpocket? "I don't think my finances, or lack of them, are any of your business."

Mallory simply smiled and tapped his nose again. Finishing his ale, he reached for the refill Becky had brought and leaned back in his chair with a gusty sigh. "The finances of other men, sir, are always my business."

Noel slid his hand into his pocket and wrapped his fingers about his pistol.

"No need for concern," said Mallory idly. His gaze flashed down to Noel's pocket, then back up to Noel's face. His expression remained bold and steady. "I work the bridle-lay only, and only when it suits me."

Noel's translator made no sense of what he said. "Bridle-lay? What's—"

Mallory laughed and rose to his feet. "Ah, you are a green one. Take care, sir, with your first visit to London town. You're a ripe gull for plucking, and the sharps will have an eye out for you."

Still laughing, he strolled away.

Glad to see him gone, Noel perked up as Becky arrived with a well-filled platter of meat and bread.

"Start yerself on that," she said, breathlessly. One of the actors across the room shouted for service and banged his cup on the table. Their laughter had gotten progressively louder, and their jokes more ribald. "I'll come back in a bit."

Noel was already reaching for a piece of the meat. He glanced up and smiled at her. "They're getting out of hand, aren't they?"

"Oh, bless ye, no. They're celebrating, that's all. Tomorrow they're going to perform for the king. It's a wondrous honor."

She hurried away before he could ask her what the bridle-lay was.

Long before she returned, he had polished off his plate. Still nursing his ale, he leaned back to digest his meal while he watched the room. To his surprise, he felt no more than mildly satisfied. Within minutes, he couldn't tell that he'd eaten at all. When his stomach growled, he set down his tankard in alarm.

There was something seriously wrong with his metabolism. He needed to talk to his LOC about it. For that he needed a room. He was still feeling exhausted. Bed sounded like a wonderful idea.

Leaving his table, he went in search of the landlord and requested accommodations.

The man, garbed in an apron and holding a collection of pipes for rent in one hand, paused in the midst of giving orders to a wizened, bowlegged hostler. He frowned at Noel and shook his head. "I got space in two beds left. The actors have filled me to the rafters. Take your pick. You want to sleep with four other men or two?"

Noel blinked. "None," he said rather sharply. "A private room, even if it's a cot, even if it's on the floor."

The landlord shrugged. "Sleep on the floor if you like. The price is still the same. There are no private rooms."

"But—"

"Look, we don't cater to the gentry. No private rooms, no private parlor. If you want to try the White Swan down the road, then—"

"No. I'll take the smaller room."

"Our best. Mr. Tuptree and Mr. Osborne of the acting company will be your companions. Very good, sir. Tommy will show you up."

Nodding his head, the landlord hurried off, and Noel was left to follow a scrap of a boy upstairs. The dark gloom was relieved only by the scrap of candle in the child's hand. The stairs themselves were steep and uneven, and Noel's legs ached as he climbed them. At the top, Noel found himself in a shadowed passageway with a ceiling low enough to brush the top of his hair. He kept a wary eye out for Robert Mallory, who might be lurking anywhere.

At the end of the passageway, the boy threw open a door and held his candle high. In the dim, flickering light, Noel saw a small room with a sloping ceiling and plastered walls. Besides the bed, it contained a table with a basin and ewer, a blackened, cold hearth in the corner, and not much else. A pair of small, much-battered trunks stood beneath the window. Boots, cloaks, and linen shirts lay scattered around in careless disarray, indicative of his fellow occupants. A stack of handbills had been tossed haphazardly on the bed, which looked lumpy and uninviting. Noel poked the mattress with one finger. It seemed to be filled with straw and was suspended on ropes tied to the bed frame. He frowned at it, thinking of a backache in the morning, thinking of lice and bedbugs, thinking of fleas and bubonic plague. He stepped back from the bed and wondered if the open field wouldn't be more sensible.

The boy lit a solitary candle on the table for him and stepped back. "Extra candles cost—"

"Never mind. One will do."

"And if you want your shoes blacked, it's—"

"No, thanks."

"There's water in the ewer and a clean towel laid out this morning."

Noel glanced at the washing table. The single towel lay crumpled where it had been tossed. Noel's frown deepened. Asking for a bath seemed pointless in these conditions. If the boy was hoping for a tip, he could forget it.

Not bothering to conceal his impatience further, Noel said, "That's all."

The boy bobbed awkwardly and left. Noel closed the door with a sense of relief that changed to uneasiness when he found out it had no lock.

Well, there was no help for it. He might as well take a chance while he had a scrap of privacy.

"LOC, activate," he said. "I need answers and fast."

"Working," replied the LOC tonelessly.

"My metabolism is off," said Noel, pacing back and forth, his ears attuned to the least sound of someone approaching. "I'm constantly hungry, no matter what I eat. I've had muscle cramps, and my fatigue level is high. Scan and make a prognosis."

"Scanning . . . heart rate is above normal, blood pressure is above normal, metabolism is burning calories at three times normal rate, lactic acid buildup in muscle tissue is above normal, red blood corpuscle level is lower than normal, with a count of—"

"Stop," said Noel, in no mood for statistics. "So what is this? Anemia?"

"Red blood cell count is indicative of anemia. However, other data is contrary to—"

"So what's wrong with me?"

The LOC hummed a moment. "Scanning." It hummed yet longer. "Scanning." After another pause, "Scanning."

"Stop. Let me rephrase my question. *Can* you tell me what's wrong?"

"Negative."

"Why not?"

"Data conclusions not within my programming."

"You mean you've never encountered this combination of symptoms before?"

"Affirmative. Memory banks do not contain this information."

"Speculation."

"I am programmed to speculate on a limited basis only."

"I know," he said impatiently. "Speculate anyway. Did this weird metabolic change of mine occur during travel?"

"Affirmative."

"Probable cause?"

"Unknown."

"Speculate!"

"Unknown."

"Damn!" Noel blew out an angry breath, then forced himself to calm down. He'd never been very good talking to computers, even those fitted with AI. The LOCs lacked artificial intelligence because that kind of programming didn't survive time travel. Why travel didn't scramble human intelligence was something the lab people were still researching. In the meantime, it meant that dealing with a LOC required compensating for its literal mind-set. And patience had never been one of Noel's virtues.

"Okay," he said at last. "I'll speculate. You follow along. Can you do that?"

"Affirmative."

Someone was coming upstairs. Noel froze, his ears listening to the murmur of voices and the laughter. The footsteps went the other way along the corridor, however. He sagged in relief.

"The last time I traveled, the time when Leon was created, there were things . . . wrong . . . with him. I'm not sure about all of it. But from what I remember and from what he mentioned now and then, it seemed like he couldn't eat or drink. Or if he ingested food, there was no taste to anything. When we were later in the emptiness of the New Mexico desert, we found out he had to be around crowds of people in order to exist. It was as though he were some kind of—not a gestalt creature—but one dependent on biological energy. He was almost symbiotic. He couldn't live alone, couldn't be a solitary entity."

Frowning, Noel paced around the room again, sifting through his memories, trying to figure out where he was going with this line of thought. "On the island, when he'd been stabbed and was dying, he held my hand and got better. He drew energy from me. He nearly sapped me, but it brought him back. We were connected. If I got hurt, he felt my pain. But if he got hurt, I didn't feel . . . that is, I didn't feel his pain but I think I somehow knew about it."

The LOC flashed steadily, its pale blue light casting more illumination in the room than the feeble candle.

"Twins," said Noel. "But not twins in the ordinary sense. We were one person until the time stream separated us. We belong back together."

"Is that a rhetorical question?"

"No." As he faced his true worry, Noel's brows knit together. "Maybe this is just a bad side effect of travel. It wasn't conventional by any definition. I'm lucky to be here in one piece."

"Affirmative."

"But am I in one piece? How can I be if Leon is a part of me and he's not here? Am I becoming like him? Is the reality of me, Noel Kedran, diminishing? Is Leon now the one who's real in this dimension? And am I the ghostly one, dependent on him?"

"Unknown," said the LOC. "To all questions."

"Or is it because we're *not* in the same time that I feel like I'm fading, bit by bit? Is that why I'm so tired?"

"Fatigue is symptomatic of more than—"

"Stop," said Noel impatiently. "This isn't simply medical. It's more complicated than that. Less obvious."

"No question has been asked."

"I *know* that," snapped Noel. "Scan for Leon. Has he appeared yet? Has he activated his LOC?"

"Negative."

"Damn," said Noel softly, trying not to let his worry get to him. "Damn, damn, damn."

Switching off his LOC, he sat down on the edge of the bed, turning his hat over and over in his hands. He had to face it. Leon wasn't here. Leon wasn't going to turn up.

Otherwise, he'd have already shown up. In Noel's previous travels, Leon had appeared immediately, within a few hours at the most, in whatever situation Noel was involved in. Well, this time, he'd been here for over half a day, and there wasn't even a hint of his twin.

Why should there be? he asked himself. He'd landed thirty-one years off the mark. What did he expect? That the time stream would obligingly pull Leon over to this date just because Noel was here?

It apparently didn't work that way.

Meanwhile, he had two more days until automatic recall. Noel tried not to remember Bruthe's gloomy comments about how perhaps recall wouldn't be possible at all. If so, then he was trapped here with bubonic plague and ignorant superstitions for life.

The prospect was not appealing.

"Ho!" shouted a voice outside a split second before the door burst open. It slammed into the wall. Two men, their arms around each other, staggered inside the doorway and stopped, swaying and blinking. One had his wig on crooked; the other wore his hat backward. Both had untied their cravats and loosened their shirts beneath their coats. The fatter and older of the pair, he of the crooked wig, raised his hands. Noel saw that the lace ruffles at his wrists were soaked through with wine.

"Ho!" he shouted again, his diction blurred but his projection loud enough to make Noel jump. " 'Carry him gently to my fairest chamber/And hang it round with all my wanton pictures/Balm his foul head in warm distilled waters—' Will! Thirsty as Hades in here. Not our room. Find us a drink."

The young man, his hat on backward, smiled sweetly at Noel and attempted a bow. "Your pardon for thish intrusion, sir. Humble apoloshies."

He attempted to turn his swaying companion around, but the two of them went on spinning around and around, unable to stop, comic in their helplessness.

The fat, older one waved his arm and declaimed loudly, " 'Hark! Apollo plays/And twenty caged nightingales do sing/Or wilt thou sleep?' Sleep, Will? You came up here to sleep in the wrong room. Man in it."

"Humble apoloshies," repeated the younger man with a second, awkward bow to Noel. "*Our* room, Mr. Tuptree. Wrong man in it." He tried to focus on Noel, blinked, and frowned. "Confound it, the man's a devil. Stand still so I can get a proper look, sirrah!"

Noel, who hadn't moved an inch after their entry, tilted his head on one side and said, "You're drunk. Both of you."

They exchanged glances and giggled together like girls.

Tuptree put a plump finger to his eye and winked at his companion. "You know, my dear Will, I believe we are."

Will hiccuped and smiled blearily.

"When drunk, my good man," said Tuptree with a grandiose gesture that nearly overbalanced him, "there is only one thing to do."

"One shing," said Will with a nod.

"One thing to do," repeated Tuptree solemnly, nodding his head with every word. "And that is to lie in the arms of Bacchus until morning. Will! There is a bottle in my trunk."

Will smiled. "Bottle in she shrunk. In she drunk. In she—"

"You will never act, Will, until you learn to enunciate under the most difficult conditions," said Tuptree. He turned to Noel, his head bobbing gently, his gaze fuzzy. "Kind and gentle sir," he said, his voice as persuasive and rich as Devon cream, "would you be so good as to find that bottle among my things and share it with us?"

In silence Noel opened one of the two trunks and pulled out the bottle asked for. Uncorked, the reek of cheap wine filled the room. He handed it to Tuptree and went to open the window.

The two actors drank deep.

"Ah," said Tuptree with a satisfied gust of air, "to quench a man's thirst is a noble deed for a wine. Were I a king, I'd knight this grape in my most profound gratitude."

Will stopped swigging and turned suddenly pale. "I feel sick . . ."

With a moan he slumped over. Alarmed, Noel sprang to grab the basin and got it in place just in time to save the floor. Disgusted, he put the bowl outside in the hall and turned around to find Will snoring gently on his side and Tuptree taking another deep swig of wine.

"The boy," he said with a small belch, his smile muzzier than ever, "is green."

"He certainly looks it," said Noel without sympathy.

"Green, sir, upon the boards. A first-season whelp, scarcely tried; his voice, sir, pitiable; his timing worse. You can hear his knees knock upon the stage. Look at him, sir. No shoulders, no calves. Spindle shanked, and a bumpkin's ignorance. Will Osborne, my dear partner's only son, my dear partner's only legacy to me after all our years in this company we put together so long ago. Can he tame a shrew? Hardly. Can he bring a dream to a midsummer's eve? Pah! Can he—"

"—know Yorick, my dear Horatio?" interjected Noel with a grin at his own pun.

Tuptree raised his brows. "I see you know Shakespeare. Are you by chance a thespian also?"

"Something like that," said Noel. "Not professional, of course."

"Ah, a gentleman." Tuptree yanked off his wig and threw it on the floor. He bowed low and ponderously. "For thee, my good sir, I shall recite one of Shakespeare's best sonnets."

"Please don't bother," said Noel.

Tuptree's mouth opened, but he looked at Noel a moment and frowned. Drawing another swig from the bottle, he offered it in silence to Noel, who shook his head.

"You are a cold man, sir," he said, his voice hurt. "Do you prefer Kyd? A lesser artist, true, but one who has appeal to the masses?"

"No, thanks. Another time," said Noel.

Tuptree sniffed. "Barbarian. I thought you of kindred spirit, sir. I see myself mistaken."

Much upon his dignity, he drank again and emptied the bottle. Cradling it to his stomach, he turned himself about and staggered around his friend, who was still snoring on the floor.

At the door, he stopped and glanced back, his shaved head looking oddly small and pointed in comparison to the rest of his corpulent body.

"Barbarian," he said clearly. "Visigoth. I do not . . . you will note that I do not say Puritan, although I feel strongly in my heart that you are one. You would keep us in the dark ages, sir. You would place shutters on our heart and iron bars on our soul. 'Thou art too like the spirit of Banquo/Thy crown does sear mine eye-balls . . . ' Silence! I will speak no more with thee. Certainly I will drink no more with thee."

Clutching his bottle and his dignity, he walked out. Noel rolled his eyes with relief, hoping the man didn't come back. Better he slept off his drunk in the taproom than in here. One was bad enough.

Reluctantly, Noel heaved Will Osborne up and tossed him on the bed. He walked over to close the door.

Just as he set his hand on it, however, he heard a cry and a loud bumping and crashing on the stairs. It was followed by silence, then people called out in consternation.

Noel hurried out with the rest to see, but he already knew what he would find.

Tuptree the actor lay at the bottom of the dark narrow stairs in a heap, unmoving, his head at an unnatural angle. He would tread the boards no more.

Casting herself over him, one of the women from the onlookers began to wail.

CHAPTER 8

Noel backed away from the head of the stairs and secluded himself in the shadows. Downstairs, the wailing and laments grew louder.

"LOC," he said softly, "activate but maintain disguise mode."

The LOC pulsed warmly against his wrist in acknowledgment.

"Scan records for an actor named Tuptree. Uh . . . at the court of Charles II."

"Found," said the LOC. "Arthur William Tuptree. Born in Liverpool circa 1621; died in the Great Fire of London, September third, 1666."

"Stop!" said Noel, startled. "What fire?"

"The Great Fire of London, originating in a baker's shop in Pudding Lane on September second. It spread across the city for five days. Most of London was destroyed, including the—"

"Stop," said Noel, drawing in his breath. "That's the day after tomorrow."

"Affirmative."

Noel thought about his trek across the city today. No wonder everything looked odd and unfamiliar. The wooden, medieval houses and ramshackle shops were due to be burned to the ground. In the subsequent rebuilding would come Sir Christopher Wren's inspired new version of the old St. Paul's Cathedral, the soaring public buildings of stone, the sturdy brick houses, the triumphal arches.

Rubbing his face, Noel pulled his thoughts back to the present. "So history hasn't been tampered with by what's just happened," he said. "Tuptree was going to die anyway. This accident is just three days early."

"Warning," said the LOC. "Anomaly warning."

A chill dropped through Noel. "No," he whispered.

"Warning—"

"How can this old drunk's death affect the future?" demanded Noel. "Was he famous? What could he do in three days to change things?"

"Before the alteration of history, Tuptree's September first performance of Shakespeare's play, *Julius Caesar*, so inspired King Charles he agreed to put aside his adviser Clarendon and continue England's war against the Dutch. Buckingham was brought in to replace Clarendon and the infamous Cabal was created the following year."

"And now that Tuptree's neck is broken?" whispered Noel.

"The play was never performed for King Charles. He continued to favor Clarendon, who remained at court as lord chancellor. Through poor advice, England lost the war and—"

"Stop." Noel scowled into the darkness, trying to think. He didn't have to get into the long and tangled political history of Great Britain to know that once again his presence in the past had opened a can of worms. If only he'd humored the old man, drunk wine with him, and listened to him spout off random lines from Shakespeare's plays. But no, he was rude and impatient. Now Tuptree was dead and history was changing.

He couldn't blame Leon for this one, he thought bitterly. He'd been the one to stick his foot into it, not his malignant twin. Leon, after all, wasn't even here.

But flagellating himself wasn't going to fix anything. Noel forced himself to think even as a man came storming up the stairs.

"Will!" he shouted. "Osborne, are you up here? Something dreadful's happened!"

He pounded on the chamber door at the end of the passageway, then thrust it open. Noel kept himself hidden and silent

in the hallway, watching as the man bent over Will Osborne
and failed to shake him awake.

"Drunk as a lord, damn ye!" he cried. "Ah, blast."

He came storming out again, closing the door with a slam,
and thundered down the stairs. Noel could hear voices con-
ferring.

"A priest? Are you daft? He won't come."

"What then? What do we do?"

"The landlord said we could put him in the pantry room for
now, till he's buried."

"But where? The sexton won't bury him in consecrated
ground. You know that, Jack."

Someone began to snivel.

"Hush up, all of you!" said Jack angrily. "It's a pauper's
grave for him. Hell and thunder, *I* can't decide. Will's the man
in charge now."

"Alas, and weep ye all for this poor prince of playwright's
art," intoned another. "Stilled, hushed in midflight as a candle
flame is snuffed out. His great voice, bell-like, to toll no more
across men's hearts. How—"

"For God's sake, Poddensby, leave off with that doggerel."

" 'Tisn't doggerel," said Poddensby, his voice suddenly
quavery with hurt. " 'Tisn't even drivel. I was thinking of
composing his eulogy. That was the first stanza, rough to be
sure, but promising—"

"Ha!" said Jack roughly. "Promising, the way you're always
promising to write a really good play for us. You can't write
your own name without botching it."

"Lads, *please*," said a peacekeeper. "Quarreling does us no
good. He's in God's hands now. Let him rest there."

"Aye," growled Jack. "He's in God's hands. But we're in
the devil's. What's to be done with us now? What about our
performance for the king? Without Tuptree we're finished.
Think on that in your prayers."

The voices quieted then and there were rustles and footsteps
as they walked away from the foot of the stairs.

Noel frowned. "LOC," he said at last.

"Acknowledged."

"Is it Tuptree that's important, or is it that the play must be
performed?"

"Arthur Tuptree was considered by contemporary critics to

be one of the finest Shakespearean actors of his day," said the LOC tonelessly. "Shall I quote what was written about the quality of his voice?"

"No. Look, if I stepped in, took his part or something, couldn't the play go on as planned?" asked Noel.

"Unknown."

"Yeah," said Noel, half to himself. "I'd have to convince them. Right. LOC, access data banks for *Julius Caesar*. Is the entire play on record?"

The LOC remained silent for several seconds, then pulsed warmly against his wrist. "Negative."

Noel let his breath whistle softly against his teeth in disappointment. "Damn. All I'd need is a portion of—"

"Condensed version of primary scenes on record in general information sector."

"It is?"

"Affirmative."

"Why didn't you say so?"

"Specific question referred to unabridged—"

"Stop," said Noel impatiently. "All I need is to memorize the main bits. Have that pulled up in ready access for when I need it."

"Affirmative."

"Deactivate."

The LOC went cold and silent around his wrist. Noel stepped out from the shadows, running his fingers through his hair and straightening his coat. Hoping for inspiration, he started downstairs in search of the actors.

However, he found the door to the taproom blocked by a burly fellow in a sleeveless jerkin and a leather apron.

"The taproom's closed."

"Yes, I—"

"There's nothing to gawk at. Go back to bed."

"I wanted to talk to the company, uh, his fellow actors," said Noel. "Express my condolences and offer—"

"That can wait until morn."

"I think not."

Noel tried to push past him, but the man gave him a rough shove back.

"You leave be!" he said angrily. "The devil's been inside this 'ouse tonight. We don't want no more trouble."

"I'm not causing trouble," said Noel. "I just want to talk to—"

"Save breath fer prayin'. Be more profitable."

Short of starting a fight, there was no getting past this oaf. Frustrated, Noel backed off and went back upstairs. Halfway up, a tight little smile curved his mouth. After all, Will Osborne owned the company, didn't he? The son of the co-founder ought to call the shots. And who was still sharing a room with Will?

Noel's smile widened.

Going into his room, he saw that Osborne lay sprawled on the bed, snoring. The candle had burned down to a stub and was fluttering. Picking up the candle and burning his fingers on the melted wax, Noel bent over Osborne and shook his shoulder.

The snoring caught momentarily, then sawed on.

"Will," said Noel. "Wake up."

Osborne didn't stir, not even when Noel shook him again.

"LOC," said Noel.

"Working."

"Scan Osborne here. Is he out for the—"

"Estimate return of consciousness in approximately eight hours."

"Out till morning," said Noel with a sigh. "Even if I throw cold water on his head?"

"It would—"

"Never mind," said Noel. He ached with renewed hunger, and since returning upstairs his leg muscles had resumed cramping. He might as well get some rest himself.

Pulling Tuptree's trunk over, he wedged it against the door. It wasn't much of a barrier, but it made Noel feel slightly more secure. Taking off his coat and shoes and unbuckling his sword belt, he stretched out on the floor, aware of time trickling by like water soaking into thirsty sand.

Without Leon here, he had to get recalled and try again to link with his twin. In the meantime, he was helpless, forced to deal with events he cared little about, repairing his inadvertent mistake, killing time while he waited to return to the future.

Killing time . . .

The archaic phrase lingered in his mind as he closed his eyes.

If time didn't kill him first.

∞ ∞ ∞

Across the city, a breath of hot wind swirled from nowhere, scattering rubbish across the streets, plucking at the skirts of a poor woman lying dead in the gutter, ruffling the hat feathers of a trio of gentlemen walking home after an evening of drink and the comforts of their mistresses, stirring the late-summer stench of the sleeping city southward across the polluted river Thames.

A solitary boatman steered his craft beneath the bridge, where the heads of the king's enemies were impaled on pikes, to rot and be pecked by ravens.

Tucked beneath one end of the bridge, hidden in the murky shadows with the soft lap of water a constant lullaby, a lump stirred slowly to life. A misshapen heart began to pump, lungs swelled with air and expelled it, a spark of cognizance formed in the brain.

Thought fragments coalesced, broke apart, then re-formed. The creature's eyes opened, but it did not as yet see. The senses delivered no input to an unreceptive brain. A numbed coldness cocooned the creature. Coldness, emptiness, a twinge of solitude so deep it was a wound.

The warm breeze stirred across the motionless figure, ruffling the garments that had rotted to tatters and thawing a little of the pervasive coldness. The day's heat, still trapped in the stone base of the bridge, radiated a soft warmth, diminished by the darkness, providing only the faintest trace of comfort.

It was the water he identified first, the soft steady lap of it, a constant sound, soothing and kind. Then he smelled it, a green, muddy fragrance, a wet scent of fish. He smelled other things as well—earthiness of ground beneath his cheek, horse dung, something sickly sweet and decaying.

He blinked and began to discern shadows. At first he saw inky blackness in contrast with hues of violet and gray, then a playful twinkle of moonlight across the surface of the river.

His breath rattled in his throat and caught. He panicked, thinking he couldn't breathe. But the moment passed, and his lungs drew air steadily again. Coughing, he fought not to choke himself and pushed at the ground until he sat upright.

He felt as old and brittle as a mummy in a case. His hands reached up to explore the contours of his face. Skin, nose, eyebrows, hair.

Whose?
No answer.
No knowledge.
Whose?

A giggle of laughter on the bridge over him caught his attention. He glanced up, listening to the footsteps echo by. He focused . . .

Aye, she's a tidy armful, all right, as trusting as a baby, her skin like velvet, God's truth, how her eyes shine in the moonlight, I could eat her she looks so fair, and she's believing everything I say, oh, sweet, sweet my reward tonight, and her father the old fool not knowing how she's slipped out, I'll have her soon, she's flushed enough, the wine helped too, and I can't believe my luck, there a good coddle of her breast, bolder than ever, and her giggling, not slapping the way she used to, aye, she's mine, all right, I could take her in the bushes I'm so randy, but better to wait, wait and make it pretty for her, she'll have me again if I do, and she's worth it, ripe and juicy and all for me.

Gone then. The thoughts and the laughter, the girl's perfume fading on the evening air like a memory.

He waited a moment longer, but all he found were his own thoughts, empty things. He struggled with them, wanting that hot, piercing clarity to return. He opened his mouth, but no sound came forth. He had forgotten how to make utterances, and yet . . .

"Woman," he said.

His voice was as rusty as a gate hinge. It hurt to speak, and yet he found himself struggling again, forcing words past the inner darkness.

"Man. Lovers. Tryst. Forbidden. Lust. I—"

He stopped, his mouth working. He sensed he had come to it, come closer to finding what he sought.

"I—I—have—I am—I *am*—I am Leon! Leon, Leon, Leon! I—am Leon. I am—Leon. Leon. I am Leon."

He said it once more, the words running smoothly in place. "I am Leon."

For that instant he knew triumph, but it was followed by no other knowledge. He dropped his chin to his chest, resting, feeling frustration wash over him anew.

"I am Leon," he whispered like a man turning a key again

and again in a lock, hoping it would open. "What does that mean?"

More footsteps on the bridge, startling him this time. Other thoughts blared in his mind: *One, two, one two one, two, damn the dark, I hate it, hate this damned pike, hate night sentry duty, no one about, thank God, but I'd like to ram this pike through a soft belly or two, just to*

Gone.

Leon blinked, his mouth open, drawing in air like a fish, drawing in knowledge.

"Soldier," he said. "Guard. Pike is . . . is weapon. Belly is target. Kill. Murder. Savage."

He shuddered, and the gate within his mind opened suddenly to a flood of images and memories. Blood and terror, the joy of seeing victims cower, the heat of battle, the cool pleasure of intrigue, manipulating, twisting weaker minds to his will, making them play as his puppets . . . so that's what he was.

He smiled, licking his lips, liking it.

"Bad," he said. "I am Leon, and Leon is bad."

He climbed to his feet, staggered a bit until he mastered his muscles, then zigzagged up the embankment to the street paralleling the river. Few lights shone out against the smothering darkness, but he could hear the citizens, snug in their beds, scratching fleas in their sleep, their heartbeats steady, their snores in chorus across the city.

People, lots of them. Stupid, ignorant, disease-ridden people. He stretched out his arms, reveling in his sense of them.

Time to explore.

He prowled the streets until he found a pair of men tiptoeing along in tall heels, silk doublets, and plumed hats. He followed them a moment, one shadow among many, listening to their drunken singing. Then he singled out one mind and put his thoughts into it: *Dropped my purse.*

"Damn," said one of the men, lurching to a halt. He began slapping his clothing.

"Whatsamatter?"

"Hell and blazes. Dropped my purse."

His companion giggled. "Aye, dropped it in that last wager. You were gaming deep tonight, my friend."

"No, I've lost it." He pulled away from his companion's hand. "Must go back and look."

"In the dark? Footpads, you know."

"I've my sword."

"You—"

"Go on a bit," said the man impatiently. "I shan't be long."

"Stupid. You can't look in the dark."

Leon bristled with impatience. The man in his power jerked with a wince.

"Faith, sir! Are you all right?" asked the friend.

"Yes, blast you! Go on. I've no need of you."

"I shall help you look, then, but it's silly—"

"I don't want you. Go home."

They parted company at last with heated words on both sides. Leon's quarry turned back and came his way, muttering angrily beneath his breath.

Leon tensed himself, waiting, then pounced and pulled the man into the shadows with him. One strong punch of his mind, and the man crumpled without a sound. Leon chuckled to himself, taking satisfaction in the ease of it, and stripped the man quickly. Bundling the stolen clothes under his arm, Leon ran.

Several minutes later, he found a house with a solitary candle burning in the window and the door unlatched. Someone was expected home. The porter who was supposed to be on guard snored in his chair. Noel drifted past him without a sound and prowled through magnificent rooms furnished with enormous tapestries, heavy, carved furniture, and fine paintings hanging in massive gilded frames.

There was a library—shadowy, firelit, and redolent of leather bindings. The cat curled near the hearth jumped up with a hiss, fuzzing itself.

Leon hissed back, and the cat ran.

Closing the door, he looked about at the tall shelves of books, the velvet cushions on the chairs, the decanter of brandy and glass waiting on the table. Tossing down the stolen clothes, Leon helped himself to a liberal glass of the brandy, then a second, smacking his lips afterward. A faint hint of smoky taste lingered on his tongue, more than he had ever tasted before.

For a moment he was puzzled, then hate filled him and he remembered the other one. The original one.

Noel.

His fists clenched and such violence filled him he nearly hurled the decanter at the wall. Barely controlling himself, he thought of that sanctimonious, sniveling coward, the *thing* he'd sprung from. Noel, the real one, who never stopped taunting Leon, who never stopped reminding Leon of who had the right to exist and who did not, who never stopped meddling.

Oh, for the privilege, the chance to get his hands on Noel's throat, to silence that voice so like his forever, to gouge out those gray eyes so like his, to cut and maim and crush until there could be only one of them.

"Me," he whispered.

He remembered the humiliation of being linked to Noel, of being jerked here and there, forced to travel through time with Noel regardless of his own wishes. Everything he tried to accomplish Noel destroyed.

But in the end, he'd freed himself of Noel. Noel had returned to his precious twenty-sixth century, and Leon had stayed in the seventeenth. Or so had been the bargain they struck.

Yet even then, there had been only treachery from his twin. Noel had gone back to safety and happiness in his own time. Leon was yanked once again from a chance at real existence, and imprisoned in *nothing,* kept *nowhere,* diminished to a speck between time streams. Noel had done that to him, had tricked him, had tried to lose him forever in the void.

Leon glared at the fire, his fingers crooked like claws, his breathing harsh. Slowly he calmed down and began to smile to himself.

Despite Noel's efforts, someone had made a mistake and let the bars of the prison down. Somehow—Leon didn't know how and he didn't care—he had escaped. He was back, corporeal, existing in the here and now. Where he was did not matter. He could survive, flourish anywhere, if left free of Noel's meddling.

Still smiling, he reached out and ran his fingers along the mantel's polished wood. Freedom . . . how the very sound of the word gave him hope. At last he could *live.*

He stripped off his tattered rags and threw them on the fire. Smoke boiled from the hearth, but Leon paid no attention. Naked, he crossed the room and put on the fine linen underclothing, the stockings, drew on the satin petticoat breeches edged in French lace, reached for the linen shirt . . . and stopped, staring in surprise at his right wrist.

A braid of silky hair entwined with gold and fitted with a

clasp circled his wrist. He dropped the shirt on the floor and touched the bracelet with a cautious fingertip, puzzled by it, half-afraid of it although he didn't know why.

What was it?

Where had it come from?

He tried to remember the last hour of his previous reality. He had been a pirate then, on a sun-warmed island, the sea wind fragrant in his nostrils. Had he taken the braid of a lover as a keepsake?

No memories came to him.

He struggled, forcing his brain to try, but there came no images save those of Noel.

He touched the braid of hair again, fascinated in spite of his wariness. He had not stolen it tonight. That meant . . . it had come from *nowhere* with him.

It belonged to him. It was his possession.

A smile touched his lips. He examined it more closely in the firelight. Strands of the hair glimmered gold and red.

"Pretty," he whispered aloud. His smile widened. "Mine."

That pleased him more than anything else. He stroked the little bracelet again, his forefinger tracing the outline of the braiding, then he frowned as darkness overshadowed his mind.

Noel wore a bracelet once. Something important about it. It had been made of hammered copper . . . no . . . silver and turquoise . . . no . . . plain leather.

Leon straightened, his mind sluggishly trying to sift through the overlap of memories. There was more, so very much more, if he could just wipe the confusion from his brain and *remember*.

But the memory he sought stayed elusively beyond his reach.

Frustrated, he turned away from the fire and finished dressing. His uneasiness grew stronger. He let his gaze rove across the spines of the books. Restlessly he poured more brandy but did not drink it.

"Always," he said aloud, struggling to put a finger on what worried him, "always I have come when Noel has come. I am here in this place and time. That means . . . *he* must also be here."

Fury filled him instantly. He whirled around, half expecting Noel to appear in the library with him, yet there was nothing but the books, the fire, and the quietness. He drew in several ragged breaths, seeking to control his emotions.

He had to think.

What was wrong with him that he could not think?

Leon paced across the room, then back again. Shifting whispers of distant thoughts caught his attention. He paused and forced himself to acquire stillness. He focused, his mind trailing the thoughts upstairs to a sumptuous bedchamber.

The clock is striking three and still he does not come home, gambling or not gambling, he hurts me, he stays away, he taunts me, my marriage vows are a travesty, yet he knows I am faithful while he samples freely, yes, freely, so many mistresses, so many lovers, I could have a lover, I'm pretty still, pretty but not pretty enough for my husband, not

Leon dropped his concentration, bored with her. The contact, however, like before, strengthened him. His mind felt sharper, his thoughts more cohesive.

Was Noel nearby, present in this time?

Leon's eyes narrowed. He'd soon find out. Gathering himself, he let his mind search across the sleeping city. Despise Noel though he might, he always had a sense of Noel's presence, like a lingering, irritating itch in the back of his throat that couldn't be reached.

He searched and searched, but no trace of Noel came to him.

Frowning, he paced the room and considered the problem. Why was he so uneasy?

It was hard to believe that Noel was not here.

He swept out with his thoughts once again, just to make sure.

Nothing.

He should have felt relieved. He should have been elated.

Instead he felt curiously hollow, almost disappointed.

His fingers reached beneath his cuff to touch the narrow braid of hair around his wrist.

Where had the bracelet come from?

What did it mean?

Why did he have such a thing?

"A key to the past?" he murmured aloud. "A key to unlock the past that I can't remember?"

The braid shimmered with an unearthly radiance. Startled, Leon cried out and stumbled back. The radiance faded, leaving only the plain braid of hair. He stared at it, half afraid of it, and half exhilarated with wonder.

"Am I a witch in this time?" he whispered with growing glee. "Am I?"

A noise beyond the library door warned him that his outcry had awakened the porter. There came a soft knock as Leon stood rigid.

"Home at last, my lord?" asked the porter's drowsy voice. "Shall I lock up?"

Leon reached into the servant's mind and took a swift image of his master's voice and manner. "Yes," he said, *pushing* with his mind to make the porter believe he heard his master's voice. "By all means, lock up."

Again the braid of hair shone with an unearthly glow of light—lambent, surreal, bathing his hand and sleeve in a peculiar pale illumination. Leon stared at it a long while until the glow began to fade again.

"Lock," he whispered, frowning.

The braid shone, and its shape shimmered and changed completely into a clear-sided bracelet filled with tiny, incredibly complicated fiber-optic circuitry. Pulsing flashes of soft white light appeared in multiple patterns.

"Working," said a toneless voice.

He jumped, and suddenly he *knew* what it was. Excitement soared through him. He could have shouted aloud, but he drew his joy down into a tiny knot of caution.

"You're a LOC," he said.

"Affirmative."

He hesitated, then touched its warm surface with his fingertip. Its lights pulsed steadily.

"A Light Operated Computer," he whispered. "Fully functional this time, not like before."

He thought of the first time he had come into existence and found himself to be a second-rate copy of Noel. He'd even had a version of a LOC, but it had been fused and twisted on his wrist, useless, mocking his own flaws.

Sucking in his breath sharply, he said, "Identify time and place."

"September first, 1666. London."

He smiled. It responded to *him*. That meant it was isomorphically designed for him alone.

He said, "Deactivate."

The LOC shimmered back into its disguise of a braid and fell silent.

"Activate."

Immediately it flashed to life. "Working."

"Deactivate."

It complied.

He chuckled and held his arm aloft while he did a jig around the room. It was his, not Noel's. He was here and Noel was not.

It meant . . . it all meant . . .

He was real.

At last, he was real. Not a copy any longer, but his own person, individual and unique.

He looked around the room, but there was no mirror to gaze into.

What did it matter? This wondrous device, this miniaturized computer with its packed data banks, represented all the reality he wanted and needed. With it in his possession, he could rule this city, this country, the world. He would be king and master of all he surveyed.

And no one could stop him from doing what he wanted.

CHAPTER 9

In the soft light of early morning, Noel awakened with a start on the floor. He lay there, tense and unmoving, all his senses alert, but heard nothing save ordinary sounds of the inn coming to life. Above him on the bed, Will Osborne still snored softly. Some of Noel's tension relaxed. There was no danger, nothing to justify the rapid pounding of his heart or the sharp sense of unease that had awakened him.

Noel grimaced to himself and sat up. His body was stiff and sore from a long night on the hard floor. He had to pry himself to his feet, and straightening his back made him wince and put his hands to his sides. He could barely walk across the room for the knots in his leg muscles. He stretched and kneaded them, trying to work them loose, and after a few minutes gained himself some ease.

The ravenous, unnatural hunger of last night had faded, much to his relief. He hoped his raging metabolism had settled down, but new symptoms had appeared, small but troubling. The inside of his mouth felt numb and tingly as though a drug had been sprayed across his tongue and the lining of his cheeks. Multiple tiny nerve twitches ran down his neck into his shoulders. He kept breaking out in a full-body sweat, although the air in the room was pleasantly cool, then he grew chilled. He checked himself for fever, but his external temperature seemed all right. Worried, he pulled apart his clothes and examined his armpits and groin for a rash or pustules. He was supposed to be fully immunized against any of the local diseases, but Ellis could have made a mistake. Maybe he was coming down with the bubonic plague.

Sticking out his tongue, he checked in the mirror but it had no furry appearance. No plague symptoms then. No flea bites, either, so he was all right in that department.

He poured some water into the porcelain basin and splashed the cool liquid on his face. It felt good and helped revive him.

He glanced at the snoring Osborne and quietly opened Tuptree's trunk, which was still positioned across the door. It contained a few items of clothing and a lifetime of mementos. Playbills yellowed with age and much handling outlined the actor's career. An oil miniature in an ornate frame showed Tuptree as a young, very handsome man before corpulence and drink had coarsened his looks. A second miniature had been painted of a young woman, lush and Rubenesque, her skin pearly white, her thick dark hair flowing free over bare shoulders. A sister? A lover? A wife? Noel laid it aside and dug further. He found a slim leather purse containing a gold crown, a handful of shillings, and some pennies. The man's life savings? Another, larger bag of frayed silk held a pearl-and-ruby-necklace. It was a lovely piece of jewelry. A third bag held a man's ring, a pair of brooches, and a lady's garnet earrings.

"Tokens of an appreciative audience," said a hoarse voice.

Startled, Noel spun around, the jewelry still clutched in his hand, and saw Osborne sitting up in bed, bleary eyed and red with anger.

"Before Cromwell's sanctimonious cutthroats killed the old king," said Osborne, "Arthur was a favorite at court. He read poetry to the queen and her ladies. He performed almost weekly."

Noel lowered his eyes from Osborne's accusing gaze. Carefully, keeping his hands visible, he put the jewelry back into its bag and returned it to the trunk. Inside he was cursing himself for not having searched the actors' belongings last night while Will was unconscious. Getting caught like this made him look like a thief. It wouldn't help him convince Will to trust him.

"Mr. Tuptree was a famous man," said Noel carefully.

Osborne's scowl deepened. "He remains famous, I'll have you know. All those years with the Puritans banning plays, closing the theaters, hunting us down like a scourge . . . well, Arthur hung on to his art. He lived in France for years. He performed for the king in exile. And when the king returned to England, Arthur knew he would perform at Whitehall again. And now he's been sent for. The lord chancellor has hired him to entertain the king tonight. It's the greatest honor of his life, and he'll be as splendid as he was when he was young. You'll see. They'll all see."

"No," said Noel quietly, closing the lid of the trunk, "I'm afraid they won't."

"What do you mean? What do you have to say about it, stranger? You're a thief. You have no—"

"I'm not a thief," said Noel, facing him. "And Mr. Tuptree is dead."

Osborne flung back the covers and scrambled off the bed to his feet. White faced, he glared at Noel. "That's a lie!"

Noel shook his head, sympathizing, but firm. "I wish it were. He fell down the stairs last night and—"

"*No!*" Osborne's eyes widened and he lifted his hands as though to repudiate Noel's words. "You're wrong. It can't—"

"I'm sorry," said Noel. "I'm afraid it's true."

Osborne staggered back and turned around. He was bone thin and narrow shouldered. From the rear he looked like a reed. He hunched over and buried his face in his hands. "Broke his neck?" he whispered.

"Yes."

"You saw it happen?"

"Heard it. I . . . I wouldn't drink with him after you passed out. He was going downstairs for more companionship when . . . it happened."

Osborne tipped back his head. "Oh . . . *God!*" he cried in despair, his voice naked with grief. "Not Arthur. Not . . ."

His voice broke into unabashed weeping.

Noel frowned and turned away, not wanting to watch, yet unwilling to leave the room. The boy sounded pathetic, his sobs ugly and ragged. His linen shirt was open at the neck and had slipped over one white, bony shoulder. With his hair standing on end, and beard stubble on his cheeks, he was a mess and should be left alone.

But Noel dared not leave. Once Will was absorbed into the grieving circle of the company, Noel would have no access to him.

Uncomfortable, he shoved his hands in his pockets and forced himself to keep talking. "They've made the arrangements, some of them, I think. They'll expect you to make the final decision."

Osborne gulped noisily and wiped his face on his sleeve. "I'm in charge of the company," he said, his voice wet and unsteady. "The director, although with me the youngest, it was Arthur they really listened to. Oh, God . . ."

"Stop it," said Noel more sharply than he meant to. "Pull yourself together. You can't face them like this."

Osborne nodded, then glared suspiciously over his shoulder at Noel. "And who are you? Why do you presume to offer me advice?"

"That's better."

"Answer my question, sir! Nay, don't bother. You're a thief. You were riffling our things when I caught you. Don't deny it."

"Sure I was going through his trunk," said Noel, making himself meet Will's eyes. "I was looking for his script."

The boy blinked. "His what?"

"His script. His part. His lines."

Will's mouth opened, then closed. He looked angry again. "Easy enough to say. We'll send for the beadle and you can tell him the same thing. Or turn out your pockets."

"The hell I will," said Noel heatedly before he remembered he was trying to gain the boy's trust. Sighing, he held up his hand to forestall Will's retort and pulled out his heavy purse of money. "Mine," he said sharply. "You can count the pittance that's in Tuptree's." He produced the wrapper that had held his lunch provided by the Institute and unfolded it to reveal a sprinkling of crumbs. Then he turned his pockets inside out and glared at the boy.

Will glared back. "Your coat?"

Noel rolled his eyes. Picking up his coat off the back of the chair, he plunged his hand into the pocket and drew his pistol.

Will gasped and stepped back against the bed. His hands lifted into the air.

"Stop that," said Noel sharply. "I'm not aiming it at you. I'm not robbing you. Put down your hands."

Will complied, but he was still pale. His gaze remained warily on the pistol until Noel put it back in his coat pocket.

"Satisfied?" said Noel. He gestured at the trunk. "Check it if you want. I've told you why I was going through it."

Will sidled cautiously around him and began to put the items Noel had scattered back into the trunk one by one, his hands unsteady but reverent as he handled them. "I suppose you haven't been through my belongings?"

"No."

"I've got heaps of plays and old manuscripts in the big trunk. Arthur never kept any. He knew them all by heart, all the good things. The rest he had me read aloud to him, then he knew his lines at once after only one hearing. He had a prodigiously good memory."

Noel said nothing. He pretended to look out the window, but he noticed when Will counted the money in Tuptree's purse, then surreptitiously pocketed it. Noel's lips tightened, but he let it go. The boy had more right to the money than anyone else. None of the actors looked prosperous.

"Why," said Will, closing the lid of the trunk at last and shoving it away from the door, "should you want a copy of his plays?"

It was the question Noel had been waiting for since he threw out the bait. He pounced. "Because I'm an actor. I want a job."

Will blinked in confusion. "Are you? But we haven't any openings—"

"Yes, you do," said Noel.

"Oh." Will's face crumpled, and tears filled his eyes.

Afraid he was going to start crying again, Noel walked up to him. "Look, I know I'm being pushy, but times are hard. You need someone to take his place, and I can do it."

"You're mistaken," said Will icily. "No one can fill Arthur's shoes."

"I don't mean I'm a better actor. I mean I can do his part."

"Sorry," said Will. "No."

"But—"

"The answer is no. We have—we shan't be hiring any-one for a time. I think I'll go home to Somerset and write for a while. The others will find work easily enough here in London."

"Hold it," said Noel. "What about your performance tonight?"

"At Clarendon House?"

Noel barely restrained his impatience. "For God's sake, yes! You're supposed to perform for the king."

"Not without Arthur."

"You can't call it off."

Will looked at him as though he had two heads. "Are you mad? Of course we will. Arthur's memory demands some respect."

"What's more respectful than to go on, dedicating the performance to him? That's what Arthur—uh, Mr. Tuptree—lived for, isn't it? To play at court again, wasn't that his dream? Are you going to throw that away?"

"But it's Arthur the king wants to see!" said Will in exas-peration. "Not the rest of this motley—"

"Where's your confidence? Tuptree trained you, didn't he?"

Will nodded morosely. "He said I was hopeless. Jack is good, but he can't do everything. Darcy has skill but he lacks the range for major roles. The others are . . . well, I couldn't afford to pay anyone better. Tuptree and Osborne isn't what it was in my father's day. My father was a genius. He penned some of the company's most popular successes, and Arthur could entrance the audience from his first word. I don't know why Arthur stayed with us after Father died. Most of the others retired or left for better positions. I've always wanted to write instead of act, but my scribbling isn't much better than my acting."

"Self-pity will get you nowhere," muttered Noel.

Will straightened his shirt and looked around for his coat and neckcloth. "I suppose I'd better go down now and face them. There's a funeral to see to, providing we can get a minister—"

"Why not?" asked Noel, puzzled. "Last night they said even a priest wouldn't come."

"I should hope not! Arthur was no Catholic."

"Yes, but why can't he be buried in—"

"Don't you know?" asked Will in a strange tone. He frowned at Noel, who shook his head. "Where do you come from, sir?"

"From a place that has no prejudices against actors," said Noel. "Do you mean it's because he's an——"

"Of course. We have the devil in us when we play a part. Our bones don't belong with those of good Christians," said Will bitterly. "A nice life, don't you think? Knowing that when you die, the vicar will send you to hell?"

"Charming superstition," said Noel drily.

A quick, involuntary grin crossed Will's face and was gone, but some of the raw grief lessened in his eyes. He clapped Noel on the shoulder. "I begin to think perhaps you really are an actor, sir. Your sentiments are in the right place. Where did you train?"

"Uh, in—abroad."

"The Continent?"

"Yes."

"Where specifically? The Druske Theatre in—"

"No," said Noel, not wanting to get into reminisces of places he'd never seen. "Mostly country fairs, small circuit. Nothing fancy. I realize you'll think I'm no good to play before a king, but I promise you I can do whatever's necessary."

Will was still looking at him in a measuring way. "Then you speak foreign languages?"

"Oh, yes."

"How many?"

"Several."

Will rattled off a question in badly phrased, horribly accented Italian. Noel replied fluently.

Will's brows shot up. "German?"

Using a Prussian dialect, Noel said something about the kaiser's mother liking ice cream.

Will grinned, but it was obvious he didn't understand. "And French?"

Noel spoke descriptively of Paris weather and the beauty of the palace gardens.

That Will did understand. He smiled. "You sound like a native. My tutor would have been rapturous over your fluency. Any others, specifically?"

"Russian, Latin, Greek, Egyptian—"

"We have no need of those languages," said Will, trying hard not to sound impressed. "You are an educated man, sir. Clever and well in funds. Why should you want a job, and with such a shabby band as ours?"

"Why put yourself down?" retorted Noel. "I can't live on my savings forever."

"From the purse you showed me you could do very well for a year or more."

"I have expensive tastes," said Noel.

"Then audition at one of the London theaters. That's why you're here, isn't it?"

"Uh, yes," said Noel. "But you're scheduled to appear at court."

"Is that it? You want to perform before the king?"

"Do I need a better reason?"

Will, however, was frowning. "You've played only at country fairs, only in Europe. No one has ever heard of you. That is, I presume as much, for you haven't told me your name."

"We were introduced last night," said Noel, lying through his teeth.

"Were we?" asked Will in surprise. "I don't remember."

"You had your wig on backward."

"Oh, yes." Will smiled sheepishly. "I've no head for drink. Forgive my discourtesy and please repeat your introduction."

"I'm Noel Kedran."

"Noel Kedran . . . no, the name is not familiar to me. So you are unknown, yet you expect to perform for the king. Without credentials, without an audition." He shook his head. "Impossible."

"So audition me," said Noel desperately.

"Not today. I have to bury my friend. If you forget the grim duty before me, I cannot."

"I know it's a bad time," said Noel, "but you can't give up this chance. Wouldn't Tuptree want you to perform?"

"You're right," said Will. "He would. It seems that while I slept you and Arthur made yourselves into acquaintances."

"Yes," said Noel softly and wished it were true. Tuptree would be alive this morning, and history would be unchanged.

"And we shall perform," said Will resolutely. He put on his coat and smoothed the rumpled lapels. "Jack will take Arthur's place. He can do a passable Hamlet. I will be Ophelia. Hal will

play the queen. He's long in the tooth but I can't do all the
women, and we fired the boys last month for . . . never mind
what pranks they were playing. Darcy will do for the—"

"Hold it," said Noel. "I thought you were going to put on
Julius Caesar."

"Impossible," said Will. "Without Arthur we have no
Brutus."

His tone held finality. Noel cursed to himself.

"I'm sorry I accused you of stealing, Mr. Kedran," said
Will. "I wish you well in your endeavors. Whether you are
a gentleman who's been cast out by his family or whether you
are spending the summer incognito for purposes of a wager,
that is your affair. But you are not a player, no matter how
many languages you speak. And I cannot admit you to our
company simply so that you can meet the king. That would
abuse the honor His Majesty has offered us. Good day to
you."

He opened the door and stepped out.

"Damn," whispered Noel, frantic for a means of convincing
him. "LOC, access *Julius Caesar*. Feed me the lines of Brutus,
Act One, through my translator implant. Quick!"

The LOC's voice filled his head. Noel listened for a second,
then jumped in, echoing what he heard:

" 'I am not gamesome: I do lack some part/Of that quick spirit
that is in Antony./Let me not hinder, Cassius, your desires;/I'll
leave you.' "

In the hallway outside, he heard Will's footsteps falter and
stop. Out of sight, Will's voice came back: " 'Brutus, I do
observe you now of late:/I have not from your eyes that gen-
tleness/And show of love as I was wont to have:/You bear too
stubborn and too strange a hand/Over your friend that loves
you.' "

Noel drew a deep breath, concentrating to be sure he got it
right. " 'Cassius, be not deceiv'd: if I have veil'd my look,/I
turn the trouble of my countenance/Merely upon myself. Vexed
I am/Of late with passions of some difference . . . ' "

He let his voice trail off and waited impatiently for a moment.
When Will remained silent, Noel strode to the door and looked
out at him. "Well?"

Will's face held uncertainty. "What is the opening line for
Brutus?"

Noel had that down cold. " 'A soothsayer bids you beware the ides of March.' "

"And his last?"

Noel swore. "What is this? The Grand Inquisition?"

Will frowned, and Noel held up a hand in apology. "I'm sorry. Uh, just a moment while I think." He waited impatiently for the LOC to scan to the end, hoping the last line was recorded in the data banks. "Still thinking. Just a minute. Oh, yeah. I'm falling on my sword in good Roman fashion. Here goes: 'Caesar, now be still:/I kill'd not thee with half so good a will.' "

He looked up, feeling like a trained dog waiting to be praised.

Will's face betrayed no expression. "How well do you know Wycherley and the works of Dryden and Etherege?"

"Not as well," said Noel truthfully, wondering if his LOC had anything on the Restoration playwrights.

Will shrugged. "So you know the lines. But can you act?"

"I can."

"Can you act before an audience?"

"Yes."

"A distinguished audience?"

"Yes!"

Will's frown deepened. "And not go blank with fright? And not let your voice break? You've had no rehearsal. We're not used to you. It's too risky, even if I were inclined to give you a chance. No, Mr. Kedran. I'm sorry."

He turned to walk toward the stairs. Noel hurried after him.

"Audition me in front of the company," he said. "Let them judge my ability to perform."

Will put his hand on the banister but paused. From downstairs came a cry: "Will! There you are at last. The most devastating thing has happened."

"I know, Hal. One moment," said Will. He glanced at Noel. "Tell me this. You are so very desperate for us to do this play. Is it a wager that motivates you?"

Noel grimaced. "Something a little more complicated than that."

"Political? Are you an intriguer? Someone from court—"

"Will!" came the shout. "Come at once."

"Please," said Noel. "I can't answer your questions. Just believe that it's very important that the play go on tonight.

All I'm asking for is that you perform it. If you need me to carry a role, I'll do it. Any role. I'm not trying to be a star here. I just—"

"Will!"

"I must go," said Will. He stared at Noel a moment longer, then frowned and shook his head. "It won't do. I'm sorry, but no."

"Wait," said Noel, but Will headed down the stairs without looking back.

CHAPTER 10

∞

Before he could figure out what he should do next, a warm pulse on his wrist caught his attention. Quickly, Noel retreated to his room and shut the door.

"LOC, activate," he said. "What is it?"

"Response to prior scanning request," intoned the LOC.

"Yes, yes? What?"

"Leon's LOC has activated."

Noel sucked in a surprised breath. "What? Repeat!"

"Leon's LOC has activated."

"Just now?"

"Activity has been running for fourteen minutes, twenty-five seconds and—"

"Stop," said Noel. He ran his fingers through his hair and paced the floor, trying to take it in. Leon was here after all, somewhere in this city. Excitement filled Noel. There was a chance now, a good chance of success . . . and return.

With a grin, he said, "Scan for coordinates. Can you pinpoint his location?"

"Affirmative."

Noel waited until he realized his LOC wasn't going to supply the answer automatically. In exasperation he thumped it. The technicians had either goofed on prep, or something had shaken loose during travel. The LOC had a pyramid memory base. It should be able to make small basic leaps of logic in spite of not having true AI programming.

A finger of worry touched him. Thus far, nothing had worked as it should. He should have traveled to 1697, not 1666. He should have connected with Leon immediately upon his arrival. He should have still been wearing both LOCs. His metabolism should not be affected this seriously. His LOC should work smoothly within its programming parameters. If all these glitches meant he was trapped in time again, he didn't think he could bear it.

Don't think about it, he told himself.

"And?" he said impatiently, prompting his LOC. "You say you know where Leon is? Tell me!"

"Latitude—"

"Stop! Translate map coordinates into a street address, the name of a building. Something *I* can find."

The LOC hummed a moment, its pulsing blue light as regular as his heartbeat. "Whitehall."

Again he waited for additional information, but his LOC merely pulsed in silence. Noel rolled his eyes.

"Whitehall?" he repeated. "Anything you want to add to that?"

"I am not programmed to desire—"

"Stop. Supply explanation of Whitehall."

"Complete or selected?"

"What do you think? Selected. Pertinent to this date only."

"Affirmative. Whitehall is London residence of King Charles—"

A knock on the door startled Noel.

"Deactivate," he said hastily, and the LOC shut down just as the door opened.

Will stood there, frowning and looking ill at ease. "Talking to yourself, Mr. Kedran?"

"Call me Noel. And, uh, no. I was practicing some lines."

Will nodded. He scuffed the floor with his shoe and cleared his throat. "We've discussed it. The others want the performance to go on."

Noel laughed aloud and flung up his hands. "Yes!"

"After the funeral, would you be willing to join us in a small capacity?"

Noel forced himself to look more serious, but he couldn't

hide the eagerness from his voice as he said, "I told you I'd be happy to play any part. I'll even shift scenery. Whatever, if you'll play for the king."

Will sighed. "I mentioned your humility to the others, and that pleased them. I . . . Hal and Jack are working on shifting the parts around. It will take a prodigious amount of rehearsal to straighten it out. I fear we won't do as well as—"

"It will work," said Noel, rubbing his hands together. "We'll make it work. Tell me what I'm to do and I'll get started while, um, while you're at the funeral."

Will pursed his lips and stared at the floor. After a moment, he asked, "Will you come downstairs and meet the others?"

Noel hurried out the door. "Of course."

Will followed more slowly, and Noel had to wait at the head of the stairs for him to catch up.

"Tell me," said Noel. "Will we be performing at Whitehall tonight?"

"No, Clarendon House. We're expected there midafternoon. To set up our props and so forth."

Frustration touched Noel. He couldn't go after Leon until he had this play business straightened out. "Right," he said with false briskness. "That sounds good to me."

He started down the stairs, but Will caught his arm. "You shouldn't be so eager, sir."

"Why not? I told you I'm anxious for a job."

"We weren't going to require you to act," said Will nervously, "but our company has thinned somewhat. Two other players left in the night. I—"

Noel smiled at him. "Don't worry, Will. I'll do whatever is necessary."

"Will!" called a man, his voice projecting effortlessly. "Stop dawdling up there. Does he agree or not?"

"He agrees," said Will unhappily. "But I haven't explained everything yet—"

"Hah!" The man advanced halfway up the narrow stairs to meet Noel. They shook hands, and Noel sized up the actor in a glance. Stalwart, with heavy shoulders and a stomach just beginning to bulge into a paunch, Jack Stewart looked to be about Noel's own age. He had long fiery red hair and blue eyes framed with long lashes. He wore a brilliant green coat that reached almost to his knees, and lace foamed at his wrists and throat. Ribbons were tied in enormous bows upon his shoes, and he wore pale silk stockings over muscular calves.

He examined Noel a long while, staring openly, and made him turn around. "Hmm," he said at last while two more actors appeared from the taproom to watch. "A bit tall, but slender enough. What think you on it?"

"Beardless," said one.

"Nothing to attract a king's fancy," said the other.

"But by candlelight," insisted Jack, "and at a distance on the stage? Draped and rouged—"

"Wait a minute," said Noel, starting to frown.

The elder of the two sighed and shook his head. "Those dratted boys. They could have stayed."

"Yes, yes, and we should have hired Sarah Coxley last summer when we had the chance instead of listening to old-fashioned Arthur," retorted Jack.

"Hold it," said Noel. "Are you trying to tell me that I'll be—"

Jack stepped past him and held out his hand. "Hal, give me your wig."

The old man, raddled about the jowls and red nosed from years of drink, blinked in affront and grasped his lapels. Puffing out his narrow chest, he said, "My wig? Poppycock! I shall do no such thing!"

"Stop being such an old blow-bag," said his companion. Without further ado, he hooked his fingers in Hal's luxurious periwig and yanked it off.

Hal's bald, pointy head was liver-spotted and he had jug ears. He gasped and made an unsuccessful grab for his property. "Damn you, Darcy! You popinjay! You shameless little scoundrel! Give back my—"

Blond and impish, Darcy danced just beyond his reach and tossed the wig to Jack, who plopped it on Noel's head.

"There!" he said. "That's more the fashion. What think you, Darcy?"

The wig was hot and smelly. Its curls lay heavy upon Noel's shoulders. He hated it immediately and wanted to pull it off and throw it back at its outraged owner.

"Zounds, yes," said Darcy, circling him. " 'Twill do very nicely. Provided he will take a more demure stance . . ."

"You!" said Jack, snapping his fingers imperiously at Noel. "I've forgotten your name."

"Kedran."

"Let us see you stand softer. Can you curtsy? Have you any artistry with a fan? Never mind. We can teach you the rudiments of that. Do you know what to do with your hands?"

Noel's hands curled into fists. Anger was pounding in his throat. He felt insulted and embarrassed. "You want me to play a woman," he said.

"Yes, of course. The role of Portia. Without the boys there's no one else," said Jack.

Noel rolled his eyes and barely held back the unwise retort on his lips. Passing himself off as a Shakespearean actor was one thing. Going out in public as a Shakespearean actor in drag was another. He opened his mouth to protest.

"I told you it won't work," said Will. "He's too old."

"But comely enough in the face," murmured Hal thoughtfully. The old actor seemed to have forgotten his anger and was gazing at Noel steadfastly.

Noel glared at the old man with fresh hostility. "Not *that* comely."

Jack threw back his head and roared with laughter. "Gad, sir, don't take affront and wave your codpiece at us. We've all played women in our day." He laughed again. "Our younger days, admittedly. We'd put Will in the part, but he's too gawky. Now will you show us a more graceful deportment, um, Kedran, or do you want a part at all?"

Noel swallowed hard, still seething. He had nothing against women, naturally, but he'd never dreamed this would happen. Why couldn't a woman play the part? Why did they all have to be men? He thought about being painted up and stuffed into a long gown, and his insides seemed to dry up and wither.

But Jack's question was no bluff. The blue eyes were steely, and as Noel met them he knew this was his one chance. He cleared his throat self-consciously, and regretted his bravado words to Will about doing *anything* in order to get a part.

Focusing his gaze beyond them, and telling himself his manhood wasn't at stake, Noel forced his stiff lips into a simpering smile, batted his eyes, and minced his way across the room.

Darcy fell into gales of laughter. Will's hesitant chuckle joined in. Noel stopped and tossed back his long curls.

Even Jack was smiling, but he shook his head. "This isn't *Taming of the Shrew*," he said. "Swing your hips like that and the king will forget he's watching a tragedy tonight."

"Yeah, right," muttered Noel, certain his face was red again. Even the tips of his ears felt hot. "It's a small but serious role. I know Portia has to kill herself and all that."

Hal was still staring at him far too fixedly. Noel glared back. Hal winked at him and Noel jumped as though he'd been branded with a poker.

He pulled off the wig. "I can do it," he said. "I gave Will my word I'd do my best, and I'll keep it."

"Well?" said Will resignedly. "Darcy?"

The blond actor was still laughing. He nodded and walked away with a friendly little salute to Noel.

"Hal?"

Hal's mouth stretched into a lascivious grin. "Of a certainty."

"Jack?"

The titian-haired actor raised his brows. "He's no worse than Timothy was. That boy was a beauty but he couldn't act worth a tinker's dam. I'm willing to risk it."

"But before the king!" said Will worriedly.

Noel opened his mouth, but neither man was paying any attention to him.

"We could write out the part of Portia altogether. Simply concentrate on the battle scenes. We're shorthanded and well you know it."

"Aye, but Portia is the conscience of Brutus. We'd better avoid the battle scenes. Too hard to stage in someone's house."

"But I think it—"

"We've spent our careers working for this chance," said Jack angrily. "And I for one don't intend to throw it away just because you've got a case of the collywobbles."

"Arthur's death deserves more respect than to be called—"

"Nonsense! The old man was past his prime, and you know it." Jack pulled a strop razor from his pocket. "I say we hire this fellow, and the others agree. You're outvoted, Will. You may as well face it and get on with the things to be done."

Scowling, Will sent Noel an unhappy glance and shrugged. "It seems to be settled."

"Thanks," said Noel. "I think."

Jack turned to Noel and handed him the razor. "Welcome to the company, Kedran. Go and shave your chest."

Noel took the razor in puzzlement. "I . . ." He caught on, and his face flamed. "Right."

Jack's laughter roared forth, and he clapped Noel on the shoulder. "Good man! Go and have a dig around in the costume trunk for anything that will fit. Mind, though, you stay out of Hal's way."

Noel felt as though he'd been scalded. "I figured that out already."

"He's prodigiously quick with a pinch."

"And I'm prodigiously quick with a left hook," said Noel.

Tucking the wig under his arm, he hurried away with what remained of his dignity, Jack's laughter roaring behind him.

CHAPTER 11

At three in the afternoon, they set out from the Horse and Crown in a pair of ponderous wagons laden with props, trunks of costuming, and the actors themselves. The sun was blinding; the air still and dusty. Road traffic clipped past them, stirring up choking clouds of dust that left them coughing and slapping their clothes.

Noel's part in the play happened to be one of those left out of his LOC's condensed version. Wedged into a back corner of the lead wagon, his tailbone feeling every bump and rut in the road, Noel tipped his hat low over his face and surreptitiously studied a dog-eared script, mumbling his lines beneath his breath in an effort to memorize them as quickly as possible.

The skinny blond actor named Darcy kicked his foot and startled him into looking up. "I thought you knew this play backwards and forwards," he said.

Noel tipped the script into his pocket and glanced around to see if anyone else had noticed. Jack and two other men lolled on top of the trunks at the front of the wagon behind the driver. They were chatting and appeared to have missed Darcy's remark.

"Nerves," said Noel with an insincere smile. "You know how it is."

"Zounds, yes. I remember my first speaking part. Years ago. How many we shall not say." Darcy cleared his throat and smiled. "I was a mere stripling and I had to play the wife of some sort of ruffian. My voice was changing, and every time it went deep I got a prodigious good laugh from the crowd. The trouble was, we were doing a drama, not a comedy. The director couldn't discharge me fast enough."

He paused a moment as though waiting for Noel to comment. When Noel said nothing, Darcy took off his plumed hat and waved it to cool his face. " 'Tis devilish hot. On days like this I thank God I'm not a ditch digger. Arthur knew the Bard himself, you know."

The non sequitur caught Noel's wandering attention. "What?"

"Amazing, isn't it? He actually met the great man when he was a boy."

"Uh, Shakespeare?"

"Of course, Shakespeare. For all of Wycherley's popularity, there's none yet who can hold a candle to the Bard. And Arthur claimed he even worked for the man, although none of us ever quite believed that tale."

Thanks to his LOC, Noel knew that Tuptree had been born five years *after* Shakespeare died. He said nothing, however.

Darcy continued, "That's why we gave old Arthur so much respect, God rest his soul."

"I thought it was because he was such a favorite at court."

Darcy shrugged and crammed his hat back on. His green eyes grew dreamy. "To be favorite to the king . . . egad, think of it! To give a performance such as would have the courtiers tossing coins and jewels at me. To bow to the king and actually be allowed to kiss the hand of the queen. I tell you, Noel, I've dreamed of this night all my life. When I was at Drury Lane I used to hold my breath before going on, praying the king would be there."

"Was he?"

"No. Still in exile in those years. We've all had our experience with exile, haven't we? Or were your relatives Roundheads?"

Noel blinked. "Uh, no."

Darcy scowled. "Those damned Puritans were worse than the plague, closing down theater after theater. I spent my best years, my rising years, on the Continent, scrounging along the provincial circuit."

He paused a moment, then added casually, "As did you, I hear."

Noel tensed, but took care not to let Darcy see it. So all this casual chatter was merely a cover for some serious probing. Noel wondered who had put Darcy up to it, not that it mattered. Whatever he answered would get round to all of them.

"As did you?" repeated Darcy.

Noel cleared his throat. "Not for long."

"Shall we reminisce? Those drafty little halls in—"

"We could compare flea-ridden inns all day long," said Noel sharply. "And if we haven't been to the same places, what does that prove?"

Darcy smiled as though confirming something to himself and glanced at the wagon behind them, where Will and most of the others rode with the props. "Frankly, I don't give a fig for whether you're what you claim to be or whether you're a courtier doing this on a dare, as Will thinks."

Noel's mouth tightened. "Nothing I say convinces him."

"Of course not. You lie very badly, my friend."

Noel looked up, and Darcy laughed.

"The devil with it," he said with an idle wave of his slim hand. "To play privately for His Majesty's pleasure is the chance of a lifetime none of us will surrender. You persuaded our pudding-heart director to let us perform, and I for one won't tip your hand."

Noel swallowed, the taste of dust strong in his mouth, and said nothing.

Darcy leaned forward, and his green eyes grew fierce. "In return for my silence, I must ask you a favor."

"Such as?"

"Give me the truth first. Is Will right? Is it a dare, some silly wager you're playing with your friends? Do you mean to flounce out in the middle of our play and ruin it?"

"I—"

"Because I warn you, sir"—Darcy's rippling voice grew thin and brittle—"our art is not something we take lightly. You see us as drunkards and clowns, lolling here on our elbows, mouthing doggerel, but when we go on we—"

"I'm not playing a game," said Noel quietly. "I won't let you down."

Darcy glared at him a moment longer, then the intensity faded from his gaze and he resumed his cynical smile. "Well, then, that's a relief. I'll say no more about it. Only . . ."

"Yes?"

"Only I hope you've taken what I said to heart."

Noel rolled his eyes. "You have my word that I mean no harm. How long is everyone going to doubt me? Till the play is over tonight? Why are you all so suspicious?"

"Things you say," said Darcy. His eyes met Noel's. "Questions you ask."

"I don't ask as many questions as I hear," said Noel tartly.

That evoked a laugh from Darcy. He gave Noel a tiny salute. "A wit, sir. I proclaim you a wit. We are cautious because old habits die hard. The Cromwell years were not kind ones. Had you experienced them as we did, you would not sit there with your eyes full of innocent puzzlement."

Noel lowered his eyes hastily.

Darcy laughed again. "Oh, that modest pose will bring Hal panting for you of a certainty."

"The hell he will."

Darcy grinned. "So let me continue to indulge my curiosity. If you are no courtier, are you a French spy?"

Noel laughed in spite of himself. "What on earth gives you that idea?"

"Your name is French."

"So?"

"You've a cursed peculiar accent. Not from the 'shires, are you?"

"Colonies," said Noel curtly, willing to say anything to shut up this line of questioning.

A strange look came over Darcy's face, and Noel felt a sudden qualm. He wasn't sure England even had colonies in America at this date.

"Virginia?" asked Darcy.

Noel sighed. "Chicago."

"Odd. I haven't heard of the place. Jack!" he called out. "Have you heard of Chicago?"

To Noel's consternation Jack broke off his conversation with the others and raised his brows at Noel. "Is that where he hails from?"

"Aye."

Jack shrugged. "North of here, I'll wager."

Darcy turned his back on the redheaded actor with a grimace. "That's Jack, full of his own importance, pretending an education he hasn't got. So tell me of this Chicago. Has it prospered as a colony?"

"Most of the time."

"Are you heir to a tobacco fortune?"

"Not that I know of."

"Chicago," said Darcy thoughtfully. "There are such odd names in America, the Indian influence, I'll be bound. Does the East India Company advertise this colony?"

"Probably not."

"And what brought you back to England?"

"Family trouble."

"Ah." Darcy nodded. "My father disowned me when I ran away to become an actor. He thought I should stay at home, marry a girl of good yeoman stock, and spend my life counting harvests."

Noel leaned back against the wooden sides of the wagon. There was no escaping Darcy's relentless questions. "My father wanted me to go into physics and mathematics."

"Like Newton?"

"Er, yes."

"I hear he's invented a new kind of mathematics. Something called calculus. The king's very intrigued by these scientists. But who knows what they will devise next. All this talk of chemistry and gravity; they sound like alchemists to me. New words for the same old devilment. Some think they're tinkering too much against the laws of nature. Bringing the plague down upon us and such—"

"Never mind talk of the plague," interjected a sallow-faced actor sharply. "Our luck of late has been ill enough without tempting Providence."

"Our luck would do better if you wouldn't botch your lines," shot back Darcy.

"Quiet, both of you," said Jack sharply. "Save your breath for your work tonight. You've deviled Noel long enough, Darcy. Let him be."

Darcy widened his eyes innocently, and looked like a satyr. " 'Twas just idle chatter to pass the time."

But the talk turned to general topics such as the recent hangings and the war against the Dutch. Noel tipped his hat lower over his face to discourage future conversation with Darcy.

His mouth was dry, as though he'd been days without water.

Despite the heat, all his sweat seemed to be centered in the palms of his hands. No matter how much he rubbed them against his legs, he could not get them dry. He'd lied to Darcy about having stage fright. No, his adrenaline surges came from the prospect of drawing closer to Leon with every plodding step of these horses. His LOC, hidden beneath his sleeve, now and then sent his wrist a warm pulse that indicated he was narrowing the distance between him and his duplicate.

He was anxious to get this mission over with and be recalled home. He didn't like the seventeenth century. His training specialities hadn't prepared him adequately for this era. Besides, although his forced layoff from missions had seemed like purgatory, he'd found that this time his travel to the past had not been the joy it used to be. The almost constant cramps in his legs hurt too much; he was tired of eating and drinking without ever feeling satisfied. His mouth remained numb inside, so numb he could barely taste his food. And the unexpected heat seemed to sap his energy.

He was more than ready to link with Leon, straighten out the rip in the time stream, and have things revert to normal. No more duplications of himself running amok, no more anomalies in history threatening the future, no more distortions, no more botched missions.

The wagons stopped at the riverbank and everyone climbed out.

Noel shoved back his hat and looked around. "What's happening? Why are we getting out?"

"We're taking the ferry across," said Darcy, jumping lightly to the ground. Dust fogged off his clothes when he landed. "Give a hand with the unloading."

Noel helped heave a trunk out and jumped down after it. "And then we load back up on the other side?"

"Aye."

"That's a lot of trouble," said Noel, struggling to push the trunk onto a set of skids so it could be dragged to the landing. "Why not just go over a bridge?"

Darcy rolled his eyes. "Zounds, but you're a lazy fellow! The bridge, my good man, is halfway across the city. And in this heat, I, for one, prefer not to inhale the perfume of rotting heads which decorate the railings. Push!"

They shoved another trunk onto the skids. The muscles in

Noel's left calf knotted abruptly. He stumbled and nearly fell. Darcy's hand steadied him.

"All right?" he asked in concern.

Biting back the urge to yell, Noel managed to gasp, "Cramp."

"Charley-horse, eh? Better walk it out in yon shade."

Darcy pointed at the graceful willow trees shading the low bank of the gentle Thames. Wiping the clammy sweat from his face, Noel limped over there, feeling both embarrassed and exasperated at his weakness.

At least it was cool under the trees. The water rippled by. Swans swam majestically a short distance away, ignoring the heavy river traffic farther out. There were barges laden with goods, little pleasure boats filled with giggling ladies and their swains, ferries, fishermen, and cargo off-loaded from the sailing ships of the East India Company and other merchants.

Noel leaned against a tree trunk and tried to massage out the cramp in his leg. Inactivity seemed to make his symptoms worse, and the ride in the wagon had probably brought on this attack. It was as though he had to keep moving constantly in order for his body to function. But activity brought on hunger, and hunger right now was giving him a mild headache.

He tried putting some weight on his leg, winced, and forced himself to stand on it. To take his mind off the agony, he pulled a hunk of cheese from his pocket and gnawed on it.

"Hollow again?" asked Jack's deep voice.

Noel turned. The slight breeze off the river stirred the actor's red hair off his shoulders. His blue eyes gazed intently at Noel, who swallowed the last bite of cheese and shrugged.

"If it's nerves that are making you peckish, 'tis a poor idea to eat. You'll chuck it up ere long."

Noel glanced past him at the ferryboat. "Looks like we're loaded," he said.

He headed that way, doing his best not to limp, but Jack blocked his path. "No hurry."

"I'm eager to get there," said Noel truthfully. "I—"

"Nay. Stand a moment. You still look whiter than Will when he waits in the wings. You *have* trod the boards before, haven't you?"

There was enough doubt in his voice to alert Noel. "Jack," he said impatiently, "I don't know how to convince you. Just believe me when I say I've done plenty of acting. I can think quickly on my feet, and I won't freeze up."

"And this rumor of Will's? I begin to wonder if he's not right."

"What? That I'm a courtier or a spy?" retorted Noel. "Why not buffoon? Or gypsy? Or smuggler? Maybe I work the, uh, bridle-lay, whatever the hell that is. Maybe I come from the moon."

Jack shrugged, but Noel's angry flippancy made his frown deepen. "We're taking a big risk professionally with you. I hope you will remember that."

"Yeah, I already got the lecture from Darcy," said Noel. "I read you loud and clear. Message received. *I understand.* All I want tonight is to see the play go on as planned. Okay? I'm not out to sabotage the performance. I give you my word."

Jack went on staring at him. "You talk as though you have a fever."

"No! I'm not sick. I'm not coming down with the plague, thank you very much. I had a cramp in my leg. I get them. It's not a portent of disaster."

Before Jack could reply, Noel swept on. "Look, I'll admit that I'm nervous. Sure. You are. Darcy is. It's natural to be hyped up ahead of time. I need that adrenaline flow, that push, so I can go out there and knock 'em in the aisles."

Jack's expression grew bewildered, and as he spoke Noel realized he was talking louder and faster, barely making sense even to himself. He forced himself to stop, and stood there breathing fast, his sweat clammy on his skin.

"You voted to let me have the job," he said, struggling to keep his words even and calm. "What's the problem now? Why all the second thoughts?"

"I do not think we can depend on you," said Jack. "There are racehorses who have plenty of speed to win, but exhaust themselves before the meet with their own nerve and spirit. They finish last."

Jack's voice had deepened with regret and something Noel could not identify. Alarmed, Noel stiffened in spite of himself. "Don't fire me now. Not this close to the—"

"Desperation is not becoming, sirrah," said Jack sharply. "Steady yourself, or by God, we'll do without you."

"I—"

"I'm sure Darcy has warned you. We do not take this lightly."

"Yes, Darcy said plenty. And so did Will. Now you. I guess by the time we eventually get there, everyone will have dropped me a word of warning. You could save time and energy by delegating one spokesman and—"

"Noel, you're angry."

"Damn right! I told you how important this was to me, and everyone acts like I don't care. I—"

Jack lifted one hand in an imperious gesture that silenced Noel. "Soft, my man, soft. If you are not what you say, then you are a very fine actor indeed."

"Well, thanks," said Noel, halfway mollified. "That's—"

"It's just that I have a very bad temper," said Jack as though Noel had not spoken. "It's not something we intend to share with Will and the others unless necessary, but Darcy has never heard of you. Never. And Darcy has been everywhere there is a stage."

He looked into Noel's eyes with a steadiness that made Noel's temperature drop a notch. "All we know of you is that you possess a certain presence which has potential, you are a prodigious liar, and you are almost insanely desperate to enter the king's presence."

"It's not what you—"

"If you do well in rehearsal and tonight's play, we'll forgive all. If you fail, and cause us to fail, then—"

"Darcy already handed out the threats too," said Noel, rolling his eyes.

Jack seized Noel by the throat before Noel realized what he was about. The squeezing pressure of his fingers cut off Noel's air and made little black spots dance in his vision. He knew a defense to break Jack's grip, but before he could swing Jack released him.

Noel staggered back a step, coughing and furious.

As soon as he caught his breath, he looked up, but Jack spoke first.

"My threats are the ones you had better fear," he said. "Get in the boat now and go back to working on your lines. Lines which you swore to us you knew."

"I—"

Jack swept his hand toward the boat.

In silence, Noel walked out to it and got in.

Clarendon House proved to be a monstrous H-shaped edifice a full three stories high. Surrounded by an ornate wrought-iron fence and a stately park of young trees, it possessed only two neighboring houses in an otherwise empty field north of Piccadilly. That is, if you could call any of them houses. They were enormous palaces, their classical, stately lines looking startlingly fresh and different in comparison to the rambling Tudor and dingy medieval architecture crammed into the rest of London. One of the three houses was still under construction, skirted by stone rubble and wrapped in scaffolding. It was going to be pretty impressive once it was completed, but neither it nor the other neighboring palace came close to the size or overwhelming grandeur of the lord chancellor's house.

Its tall windows glittered in the hot sunshine of late afternoon, and as the wagons bearing dust-coated actors, trunks, and stage props rolled ponderously through elaborate entrance gates Noel stared with amazement at the building towering beyond a vast courtyard. The whole Time Institute could have fit in a third of this building, which had to rank among the most stately, beautiful examples of architecture he'd ever seen. The little domed tower in the center of the roof spoke of Palladian influence; a classical stone balustrade bordered the entire roofline. The front steps seemed to rise forever to the door itself.

Noel imagined stepping through that door into an entry hall filled with fabulous artwork and treasures, with bowing servants to welcome them with cool drinks. Instead the wagons rolled around to the side tradesman's entrance, where an irate servant in livery scolded them for getting in the way of the delivery carts still unloading provisions for the evening's banquet.

From there it was all chaos. The king had not yet arrived, but courtiers and their ladies pulled up in their carriages in a steady stream. Each arrival was marked by a flurry of servants, barking lapdogs, conflicting orders, shrill voices, and a hastening of silk and petticoats upstairs. In the multitude of guest chambers they would change into their finery for the evening. The upstairs servants were kept hopping to receive the guests and accommodate their constant requests; the downstairs servants worked furiously to finish preparations for the evening's lavish entertainment.

"But we're expected," said Will to the pockmarked footman blocking their way. "Tuptree and Osborne Company of Players. We were hired for this evening's entertainment."

The servant raised his brows and looked unimpressed. "Wait here," he said sternly. "I shall inquire."

There was stuffy coolness in the basement, where innumerable servants of both sexes came and went hurriedly. The actors huddled in a sort of antechamber just inside the tradesmen's entrance and watched sturdy men in breeches and leather aprons carry in casks of wine, sacks of flour, great haunches of meat, baskets of fish, barrels of candles, and bundles of fresh vegetables. Dapper individuals dropped off clothing straight from the hands of the tailor. A tobacco shop delivered freshly ground snuff, mixed and scented to His Lordship's order. The musicians arrived at the same time as the cut flowers. A barber and his assistants appeared and were whisked away by a valet. Hairdressers laden with boxes of accoutrements, their flunkies carrying elaborately curled wigs on wooden stands, passed through babbling in French.

The footman returned. "According to His Lordship's secretary, you are to perform outdoors on the terrace tonight."

The actors shifted and exchanged unhappy looks. Noel wondered what was wrong, but he didn't ask. No one had spoken to him since Jack had throttled him in front of everyone, and he wasn't in the mood to mingle. While Will tried to argue with the footman, saying that their voices would project better indoors, Noel edged across the small room and peered down the corridor beyond.

The disguised LOC on his wrist had been pulsing with increasing force since they crossed the Thames and now it was a constant circle of warmth against his skin. Leon was here, somewhere in this massive palace. Like the divining rod of a water witch, Noel could feel a curious tuning within himself. It was magnetic in force as though nature—or time—were itself pushing them toward each other. He had to find Leon *now*.

He took a step forward.

"Noel," said Jack. "Come on this way."

Startled back to an awareness of his surroundings, Noel looked around and saw the actors following the footman away like a flock of sheep. He fell into step, although it was difficult to make himself stay with them. His concentration kept unraveling at the edges of his mind, and he had to force himself to remember he had other business besides Leon.

The basement was filled with humid, soapy air at one end. Laundry women, their cotton dresses sweated to their backs, took down vast white tablecloths from a ceiling-high drying rack. They held the cloths off the floor while more women ironed them section by section. Little girls in mobcaps ran back and forth every few minutes to fetch them freshly heated irons from the fire.

At the other end of the basement, exquisite scents of cooking made Noel's mouth water. Long pine tables heaped with vegetables were surrounded by scullions with paring knives. Another table held freshly plucked birds, their naked skin pimpled as though cold. The chefs screamed orders at minions. Copper caldrons bubbled over the fire in one section of the kitchen, while in another the pastry cook carefully iced tiny cakes in the shape of white swans.

"I'll show you where the terrace is by the most direct route," said the footman.

"What about our props?" asked Jack.

"Those can be carried round through the gardens. Mind you disturb none of the guests. Come this way, and touch nothing."

Mouthing insults to his back, the actors followed their snooty guide upstairs to the ground floor. Noel looked around as he walked, his head swiveling to see all the magnificence. His initial sense of nearness to Leon had faded, although the LOC remained warm on his wrist. He drew a deep breath, telling himself to be patient.

Half-open doors provided Noel with glimpses of chambers beyond imagining. The dining room itself was vast, lined with innumerable chairs of crimson damask. A servant crawled on his hands and knees across the endless expanse of table, polishing with beeswax as he went.

"Come along. Don't dawdle," said the footman, and Noel hurried to catch up.

They walked through the central entrance hall, which was hung with magnificent tapestries and portrait oils by Lely, Van Dyck, and other masters. Light from the upper-story windows flooded the broad wood-and-marble staircase.

At the back, they were led through a spacious salon fitted with priceless carpets, marble busts of the great philosophers displayed in wall niches, hand-carved mahogany furniture, and a ceiling painted with a mythological scene of rosy-tinted women pursued by cupids and eager suitors.

Trying to gawk and walk at the same time, Noel followed the others outside through french doors onto the terrace. Stone steps led into the gardens, which covered several acres. The plantings were young and incomplete in places, including a maze that was only waist high.

Laughter in the distance caught Noel's attention. He saw women in long dresses sitting on benches in the shade, their fans moving languidly as they watched a stylized game of hide-and-seek. Men in outlandish outfits of periwigs, plumed hats, plentiful lace, and high-heeled shoes minced around them. The men bent low to steal kisses behind the fans or enticed the ladies out of sight into long shady arbors strewn with fallen rose petals.

Those playing hide-and-seek kept shrieking with false outrage and chasing each other into the shrubbery.

"Noel!" said Will sharply. "There's much to be done."

But Noel paid no attention. He walked to the edge of the terrace and leaned on the balustrade near an urn filled with blooming flowers. Like a scent that filled his nostrils, he felt it hit him, some surge of focused awareness such as he'd never experienced before. He looked until he saw a bewigged figure flirting in the distance, a man slender and dark headed, a man that made the hair rise on the back of his neck.

He stared, squinting in an effort to be sure.

"Noel!" said Will again. "We have to—"

"Excuse me," said Noel. "I have to take care of this."

He started down the steps, but someone caught his coattails and pulled him back. Turning, Noel found himself face-to-face with Jack. The actor's blue eyes were narrowed with anger.

"This is no party for us, Kedran," he said, his deep voice low but holding an edge. "We didn't give you this job for you to go gandering among the gentlefolk."

In spite of himself Noel's attention wandered back to the distant courtiers. He was too far away to see the man's face clearly. But something in the set of his shoulders, his stance, and the way he moved as he reached down and took a curling lock of the giggling woman's hair in his hand . . . Noel could feel his stomach drawing tight with tension.

"Hear me!" said Jack, giving Noel's sleeve a yank. "You'll keep your place and do what you're told. Is that clear? Or do I have to give you another lesson in concentration?"

"But I think I know that man over there—"

"No matter. You'll work, sir, or you're out."

Noel swung his gaze back to Jack's and met him glare for glare. He could feel something in him humming with recognition, reaching forth for his duplicate, his other half. He forgot about the importance of the play, forgot what he'd promised. It was Leon he needed now, needed and desired as he never had before. He could feel an ache, something just short of actual pain, spreading through him, leaving him hollow inside and vulnerable.

"Without me," said Noel to Jack, "you're shorthanded. Or have you forgotten?"

Jack's face darkened. "By God, we'll do without you if we must."

"Then go ahead," said Noel recklessly and hurried down the steps.

Behind him he heard Jack and Will arguing, but he paid no attention. One of them called his name, but he didn't glance back. Neither of them dared follow him, but as he reached the bottom of the steps, he quickened his pace until he was almost running.

It was Leon, all right. Leon, his mirror image, the creature cloned from him in a past journey through the time stream, an evil, degenerate duplication that both repelled and fascinated him. He had returned to the past to find Leon, and to rejoin with Leon.

Now . . .

Leon was still flirting with the giggling woman, taking her fan from her fingers and stealing quick caresses of her semi-bared breasts with an audacity that had her panting. She was petite with dainty hands and feet, her plump figure curved in all the right places. Soft brown ringlets spilled to her shoulders. She wore a quantity of pearls, and her tightly laced gown was fashioned of coral silk and old lace.

She saw Noel's approach and blushed rosy pink, but she did not stop Leon's roving hands. Leon's back was to Noel. He leaned over and kissed the lady's ear. While her eyes were half-closed he boldly removed the pearl and diamond dangles from her ears and put them in his pocket.

Her eyes flew open and she rapped his shoulder with her closed fan. "Fie on you, sir. Taking my ear bobs. Give them back."

Leon's fingers caressed her cheekbones. "But you have such delicate, perfect ears," he said in a husky but compelling voice. "To adorn them with jewels is to desecrate them."

His hand lingered on her cheek, and Noel saw her eyes flutter and lose focus.

She said drowsily, "But my . . . my husband gave . . . they're family heirlooms . . . very . . ."

"You lost them somewhere in the arbor," said Leon. "You will have all the servants look for them later."

"Later," she repeated.

Noel tapped Leon on the shoulder and made Leon jump. "What a crock," he said angrily. "Give the earrings back and stop messing with the woman's mind."

Leon's face went wild with rage. His pale silver eyes narrowed, and madness filled them until he drew a deep breath and regained control. His fists clenched at his sides.

"*You,*" he whispered with loathing. "Here—"

"Yes, here," said Noel. He looked past Leon at the woman who was sitting in a trance, her face slack and vacant. "Release her and send her away. I've got to talk with you."

Leon held up his hand in flinching repudiation. "Never again! You're not real. I'd sense you if you were."

Noel gripped his hand and forced it down between them, feeling the strength in Leon bunch and strain against his own. "I'm real," he said. "I've come for you."

"No!"

"Listen to me," said Noel urgently. "The fabric of time is coming apart. We have to reenter the stream together, return to being one—"

"No!" Panting with exertion, Leon broke free of Noel's grip and glared at him. "You gave your word I could live here."

"I left you thirty-one years into the future," said Noel. "But you didn't stay there."

"What does that matter?"

"It's just another indication of the growing instability of

time. You and I are . . . are part of a whole." Noel frowned, reluctant to say it aloud although he'd been trying to accept it for quite a while. "We can't be apart, no matter how much I'd like to leave you forever."

Leon's eyes shifted rapidly. He was pale and sweating. His hands reached up as though to claw his face, then stopped. He shook his head. "You gave your word," he repeated hoarsely. "I'm real now. I deserve my own life."

"No," said Noel. "That's the problem. It can't work."

"It can if you will leave me alone!"

Leon tried to hurry away, but Noel blocked his path.

"Listen to me," he said, trying to get Leon to look at him. "When I returned to the Institute, to the twenty-sixth century, I thought you would remain in the seventeeth."

"Liar!"

"You didn't. We monitored you on the—"

"Bastard! You had no right!"

"You lost corporeal cohesion as soon as I left," said Noel. "Your wave pattern scattered and we could barely track you. You were nonexistent while I was gone. Just a speck of consciousness between dimensions."

Leon backed away from him, his shoulders hunched, his eyes still wild. "You lied to me."

"Why should I lie?"

"Because you hate me. You want to destroy me." He held up his right arm and pointed to the braid of hair encircling his wrist. "I have this now. I'm just as good as you. Better! And you can't stand that. You want to—"

"I'm trying to help you, to help both of us."

"Liar!" cried Leon, still backing away. He bumped against the woman on the bench, and she toppled over in silence, her face and eyes still empty while she waited for Leon's next command.

Noel pulled her back up to a sitting position, handling her slack limbs like positioning a doll, then hurried after Leon, who was striding away. He caught Leon's arm and spun him around. "You're deliberately misunderstanding me. I don't want to destroy you. I want to integrate you."

"Same thing."

"No—"

"Same thing. Same thing!" cried Leon hysterically. He

backed into a bush and fought it off as though it had attacked him.

Noel caught his arm again, and he flinched as though he'd been struck.

"Get away from me!" he said hoarsely. "You're a monster. You want me to be like you. You want me to die."

"We're two parts of a whole," said Noel. "God knows I don't want your nature mixed with mine, but that's where you came from. I have to accept it. I—"

"You," said Leon with a sneer. "You, you, you! What about me?"

"You care more than you'll admit," said Noel. "Remember the pirate ship, where you saved my life?"

Leon threw his head back and laughed, but the sound rang hollow with desperation. "And you think my motives were kind? You think I honestly cared a damn for whether you lived or died?"

"You can't deny your actions," said Noel, thankful he finally had his twin's attention. He forced his tone to be gentle. "You took the knife meant for me. And you nearly died."

"I pushed you out of the way because if you'd died then I would have too," said Leon. His face twisted in a grimace. "Back then I was connected to you. I could feel you. I had to experience sensation through you. If you hurt I hurt. If you died, I . . . died. I didn't intend to be stabbed in your place. I was simply pushing you aside."

"Liar," said Noel softly, almost affectionately. The emotion surprised him, but he smiled just the same and reached out his hand. "Rationalize it all you want, but the feelings cannot be denied."

"I tell you it was self-preservation, not any concern for your skin," said Leon angrily. He stepped toward Noel. "I had to protect you in order to protect myself, but I'm not what I was. You let me fade when you left for the future. You put me in that limbo of hell. I went mad there . . . and yet I returned. I am whole now. I am alive. I am separate. I can taste food by myself. I no longer sense your presence. And I have a LOC that obeys me and only me."

"I brought that for you," said Noel.

Leon sneered. "Then why was it on my wrist when I materialized here? Why is it not in your hand now, to give to me?

Your lies grow more tangled all the time, brother dear. But know this, I am no longer a part of you, will no longer be linked to you. The hold you had over me is gone. I am free, and I intend to stay that way."

"Leon, you have it all wrong."

"Do I? Then let me demonstrate it in a way you'll understand."

As he spoke, Leon reached into his pocket and drew a small dagger. That was all the warning Noel had before Leon lunged at him. Noel tried to duck inside his reach and deflect the blade, but he was a fraction too slow. He felt the tip of the knife point scrape across his chest and bite deep into his right shoulder.

With a loud, ecstatic cry Leon put his weight behind the blade, driving it deep. Noel stumbled back, felt his knees buckle, and sank.

Leon stood over him, his legs braced apart, and held the dagger steady as Noel slid off it and collapsed on the ground. Air rushed into the wound then, and the pain was so intense it seemed to rob him of breath and stifle him. He couldn't make a sound, couldn't comprehend anything except the agony and the hot scent of blood. It gouted from his chest, and he felt his life flowing out with it.

He twisted onto his side, trying to put his hand on the wound, trying to stop the blood. But breathing was too hard. Moving was too hard. He could hear a roaring in his ears. His vision grew blurred and smoky. Leon tossed the bloody dagger aside into the bushes and continued to stand over him. He was laughing, but Noel could not hear the sound for the gurgle and thrash of his own blood within his ears. *Lung penetration*, he thought. *Drowning* . . .

Noel's eyelids blinked, stayed down, and dragged open only after a struggle. He found Leon crouched by him now. Leon's fingers dug into his arm. The lace at Leon's wrist was stained crimson with Noel's blood, but Leon did not notice.

"Now you know," he said, and although his voice sounded very far away, his words were distinct. There were screams in the distance, a woman's screams. "I want to tell you that I feel nothing, not a twinge, not a hint of your mortal wound. Die alone, Noel, for I am no longer a part of you."

Rising, he turned and strode away into the arbor, leaving Noel to fade in the dust.

CHAPTER 12

The sun was setting when the king finally arrived. A fanfare of trumpets sounded as his entourage of carriages and outriders swept through the gates of Clarendon House. Servants hurried to throw open the doors, and Lord Clarendon himself, sweating beneath his long wig, hastened forth to greet his sovereign.

Leon, decked out in clean, extravagant lace and cloth of gold, positioned himself among the fluttering courtiers and waited like a cat for his prey. Around him, the heartbeats and quicksilver thought-flashes of the others were no more than white noise, a distraction that he shoved away. He had already pinpointed the king's mind from the others. As yet, he had not touched it. He waited for the right moment, his impatience throbbing beneath an exterior of false calm.

While his eyes remained focused on the man emerging from a gilded carriage adorned with plumes at each corner, Leon's own thoughts kept sliding back to Noel. A smile curved his lips and he felt joy bubble inside him. He wanted to hum; he wanted to skip and clap his hands. Instead, he shook back the lace at his wrist and admired his disguised LOC. After so much fear and worry, the deed was done. Noel was dead.

Leon's smile widened. He tucked his chin low into his cravat and chuckled to himself. He felt deliciously wicked. He felt as though he could stride the world tonight and be back by dawn.

He had never felt more alive, more whole. He should have killed Noel long ago. Fear had held him back, but he would never be afraid again.

A whisper ran through the courtiers. "The king! The king!"

The awe in them filled the hall like humidity. Leon returned his attention to the tall dark-haired man now striding up the front steps.

Charles was bigger than Leon expected. Broad-shouldered, with a long, rangy stride, he walked in the midst of a swirling, yapping pack of tiny cavalier spaniels. He was dressed in maroon silk that complemented his dark coloring. His face had been famous for centuries—hardly handsome but not unattractive. From the information in the LOC's data banks, Leon had learned that the king tended to be lazy and tolerant. He liked wine, women, and gambling. And although he couldn't afford the latter, the first two pleasures had given him quite a bawdy reputation.

Leon was prepared to find this man a dissipated puppet. Instead Leon found himself surprised by the king's alertness, intelligence, and presence. In real life, his dark eyes held a brilliance that commanded instant respect. His expressions were animated and constantly changing as he greeted his bowing host, gave him an affectionate clap on the shoulder, and continued chatting with Clarendon as they both entered the house.

Around Leon, the courtiers bowed. Leon's back seemed fused at first, but a tug on his coattails made him bend in an awkward bow at the last moment.

Charles's gaze noticed the near-insult and he paused. Glancing up in direct violation of protocol, Leon gathered Charles's mind within his and *pushed*.

There was more resilience than Leon expected. Not everyone could be bent to his will, and it enraged him that this king might be one of them. Leon *pushed* again, harder. This time the king's mind gave way to his. For a moment the king's face went slack, and his dark eyes grew dull.

"Your Majesty?" said Clarendon in concern. "Is Your Majesty well?"

"*I am Leon Nardek, a dear friend of your exile,*" commanded Leon to him. "*I am your favorite at court. You have not seen me in many years, and you are delighted at my return to England.*"

"Your Majesty?" said Clarendon again. He dared touch the king's sleeve. "Is something wrong?"

The animation surged back into the king's face. He blinked, and his dark eyes smiled warmly into Leon's. Ignoring Clarendon completely, he held out his hand to Leon and said, "Why, Leon, our dearest old friend. What a wonderful surprise. How charming to find you here. When did you return to England?"

Shaking the king's hand, while those around him nearly swooned with envy at this tremendous favor, Leon grinned. "Only yesterday, Your Majesty. I've been away a long time."

"Far too long," said the king. "Why did you not write to us? We have wondered about you so very often."

"Your Majesty honors me," said Leon modestly, while inside he gloated at the confounded expression on Clarendon's face.

"Honor nothing!" said the king with spirit. He took Leon's arm. "We are agog to hear all your news. We must catch up on what has transpired since last we saw each other. Wine, Clarendon! We would toast to old times with our friend."

"Uh, certainly, Your Majesty," said Clarendon. Still looking astonished, he snapped his fingers at a servant. "I beg Your Majesty will indulge me by touring the main rooms while we wait for refreshments?"

"Hmm?" said the king. "Must we?"

The wounded look on Clarendon's plump face made the king's impatience soften. He dropped Leon's arm and nodded to his lord chancellor. "Yes, of course we must. We are letting ourselves forget the obligations of a guest. Very well, a tour, sir."

Clarendon bowed. "Your Majesty is most gracious."

He led them off into the grand salons, but almost immediately the king had turned back to Leon to ask him yet another question.

The astonished court followed like sheep, murmuring among themselves. Leon reveled in the king's eager questions, feeding suggestions into the king's mind as needed, making himself right at home.

In fact, he rather liked this house. He had examined it thoroughly during the afternoon before Noel arrived and started causing trouble. And although his LOC said the house was destined to be torn down within a few years, Leon had no intention of letting that happen. He felt the palace suited him, and now, feeling reckless and successful after having disposed of his twin, he tossed his initial plan of gaining a place at court. Joining the ranks of fawning courtiers was not for him. Why should he wait? The sooner he got rid of Clarendon, the sooner he could move in.

Therefore, he kept the king so charmed with his chatter that Charles barely looked at the splendid treasures on display. Down in the muddy depths of the king's mind, Leon unearthed a faint hint of displeasure that Clarendon should have spent such a large fortune on this new house while the king was still having to beg Parliament for money to cover his own debts. Leon probed that tiny spot, making it sore.

It would be very easy to unseat Clarendon in the king's affections. The lord chancellor was unpopular with the people. This new house that he was showing off had made him even more disliked. After all, he had taken the stone meant to repair the old and crumbling St. Paul's Cathedral and used it to build this palace. While the king suffered from a cloying loyalty to this fat old man who had stood beside him for so many years, Leon knew how to get around that.

Lord chancellor . . . he rather liked the title. It would be a good place to start. He could run Charles and, through him, the country. After all, Charles was already proving to be a lot of fun. Several of the ladies present this evening had sparked some truly licentious trains of thought in the king's mind, and Leon reveled in these dark tastes of voyeurism. It was almost like old times, sharing Noel's experiences through his twin's emotions.

But the thought of Noel darkened Leon's pleasure. He frowned to himself, impatient at his own memories. Noel was gone. He didn't want to think about his twin. He was rid of him forever, and he liked it that way. From now on, he would eat, drink, and be merry on his own, for himself. The king and his bawdy court would provide ample opportunities.

Charles was a lazy man who liked his pleasures. He would rather hand over generous sums of money and high titles than endure unpleasantness. Leon knew just what to do with those attributes.

He smiled to himself. As long as Charles remained useful, Leon would let him think he was still king.

And this time, he thought, as he found himself seated at the magnificent banquet table in the place of honor at the king's side, there would be no Noel to interfere or to change history or to yank him away from what he created here.

Touching his wine goblet to the king's in a mutual salute, Leon tipped back his head and drank deep.

CHAPTER 13

A dim room . . . essence of mold and damp . . . furtive whispers of sound like dry leaves . . . Leon's sneering face floating tethered to the farthest reaches of the subconscious . . .

Noel awakened slowly, aware that he'd been semiconscious for some time, but unable until now to break through to full awareness.

He was lying on a narrow cot, very hard and uncomfortable, in a windowless room lit only by a candle burning on a small, homely table. The room contained a chair and a small chest for clothing. It smelled musty and unused.

Blinking, he rubbed his face with his left hand and slowly pieced things back together. The right side of his chest hurt, the painful throb of its beating subdued beneath the medication in his bloodstream. That, he knew, was courtesy of the emergency programming in his LOC, which automatically sensed any sudden or significant drop in his vital signs and could administer an injection to his wrist.

The same information was supposed to be relayed back to the Institute, which was supposed to perform emergency recall in case a traveler was injured.

Noel gingerly probed his bandages and winced. The knife had apparently gone in where his heart would have been, had he a heart on the right side *as Leon did.* For once he was grateful Leon did not always think with all cylinders.

No recall . . . he forced down an involuntary spiral of panic. This wasn't like the last time, when he'd been trapped in medieval Greece, terribly injured, and couldn't get back. Then his LOC had been sabotaged; this time was different.

At least he hoped it was different. If he kept letting himself be paralyzed by memories of what had happened before, he'd never get his confidence back.

The fact that he was still here meant several things. One, he wasn't injured seriously enough to alarm the LOC's sensors. Two, he wasn't with Leon, and they had to reenter the time stream together for this to work. Three, the alteration in history that he'd inadvertently caused had not been corrected. It was possible that right now no Institute existed to return to.

He tried to swallow, but his mouth was so dry his tongue kept sticking. That damned play . . . how important could it be?

"LOC," he whispered, keeping his ears attuned to the low murmurs outside his door. "Activate."

The LOC flashed to life. "Acknowledged."

"*Shush!*" he said. "Lower response volume. Generate a damping field as protection. Freeze the hinges of the door so no one can come in until I'm finished talking to you."

"Working . . . ," said the LOC much more quietly. Its blue light flashed briefly, creating odd shadows in the corner of the room. "Protection established. Security systems operational."

"Good." Weakness washed through Noel without warning, leaving him dizzy and sapped. He fought against the temptation to close his eyes and slip back into darkness. "Run . . . run prognostics," he said weakly. "What is my condition?"

The LOC hummed busily. "Vital signs are—"

"Stop," he said. "Don't give me anything technical. How much blood have I lost?"

"Three pints, seven ounces."

"What?" he said in startlement. "Impossible. I wouldn't be able to—"

"Blood is being replaced in cardiovascular system at a rapid rate," said the LOC. "Cell division is seven times normal rate; tissue is being repaired at—"

"Stop," said Noel. He frowned in growing puzzlement, not certain he liked what he was hearing. "Let me get this straight. You're saying that I'm already healing?"

"Affirmative."

"But that's impossible. I can't heal that fast unless I'm between dimensions, traveling through the time stream itself."

"Affirmative."

"But I'm . . ." His voice trailed off as an awful suspicion occurred to him. "Have I traveled while I was unconscious?"

"Negative."

"I'm still in 1666?"

"September first, 1666. London, England. Eighteen hundred hours—"

"Stop." Noel tilted his head back and rested a moment, trying to sort it out. The bout of dizzy weakness had passed, but he still didn't feel as though he could jump out of bed and dance the minuet. "Explain why I'm healing so fast."

The LOC flashed a moment in silence. "I am not programmed to respond in that area."

"Why? Lack of data?"

"There is no recorded information on this phenomenon."

"Speculate then. Does it have something to do with my metabolic rate being abnormally high during this travel?"

"Probability is ninety-one percent."

"And we don't know why my metabolism has been affected this way."

"I am not programmed to respond to rhetorical questions."

"No one asked you to respond," snapped Noel. "That's why it's called rhetorical."

The LOC said nothing, and he glared at it until the hammering of his heart and a sudden shortness of breath made him force himself to calm down. Getting mad at the computer accomplished nothing. He had to conserve his energy.

"LOC," he said, "at present rate of healing, how long until I'm back on my feet?"

"Precise—"

"No, approximate estimation is fine."

"Approximate estimation is one hour, forty-five minutes."

Noel couldn't contain his astonishment. His mouth fell open. "You're kidding."

"I am not programmed to—"

"Yeah, yeah, I know that." He turned the idea over in his mind and found it unbelievable. "In less than two hours, I'll be as good as new?"

"Negative," said the LOC. "Original question was—"

"How long until I'm back on my feet. All right. You're literal, and I'm not. So I can still perform in the play if I have to."

"Affirmative."

Noel touched his bandages again and flinched. The wound was just as sore as ever. If the LOC didn't have a knot in its optic fibers, then at this rapid rate of healing he should be able to *feel* himself getting better. He started to query the LOC further, but changed his mind. He could chase the computer around all night and not get better answers.

Plenty of things had gone wrong with this trip. Starting with how he'd gotten here. As long as he lived he wouldn't forget being sucked by the distortion into the vortex. Then he'd landed on the wrong date. The spare LOC that he was supposed to give Leon had detached itself in the time stream and gone to Leon on its own. That was pretty damned weird, all by itself. Then his body was all messed up, running at too fast a rate, burning too much fuel, exhausting itself, healing itself. And Leon . . . Leon wasn't a piece of him anymore. Leon, now that he looked back on his encounter with his twin, had seemed more vibrant, more alive than ever. It was almost as though Leon were the original and Noel had become . . .

"The copy?" he said aloud.

Horrified, he struggled to sit up, felt a fresh onset of dizziness, fought it off, and balanced himself on the edge of the cot. The floor tried to rush at him, but then it backed off. He sat motionless until everything looked normal again and wiped the clammy sweat from his face.

"LOC, could it have happened?" he asked softly, almost too frightened to utter the words. The concept itself was terrifying. "Could we have reversed in the time stream?"

"Unknown."

"Not reversed," he corrected himself. "Because then I'd be right handed and he'd be left handed. But . . . I guess I'm looking for a word like . . . inverted. Yes, inverted. Our roles somehow switched. Is it possible?"

"Unknown."

His mouth twisted. "Great. You're a big help."

The LOC flashed steadily, oblivious to his sarcasm.

Noel chewed on his theory. It was farfetched, sure, but then so was everything. And it made sense. In fact, it was the only theory that could be stretched to explain everything that had happened so far. It also explained why he couldn't seem to accomplish what should have been a simple mission.

"The copy," he muttered again, staring at his hands, which were resting on his knees. They looked the same. He saw no changes. No external changes, but would he know?

His thoughts skittered away from that one.

"LOC," he said. "What happened after I passed out?"

"Summarization," replied the LOC. "Jack, Will, and Darcy rushed to your assistance. They carried you from the garden and brought you here. Your wound was cleaned and bandaged. Some attempts to rouse you were unsuccessful due to my protection intervention."

"Thanks."

"You are welcome."

"Then what?"

"They left to discuss what had happened and to decide how to keep the matter quiet. They are in great emotional turmoil, worried that they will lose their employment."

"It's a big deal for them," said Noel absently, "performing for the king and all. Did they say they were going to cancel?"

"Unknown."

"Okay. I'm not critical to the plot line. As long as they perform *Julius Caesar*—"

"Discussion included a change of—"

"Change the play?" said Noel in alarm. "No way! To what?"

"Unknown."

"Damn." Noel ran his fingers through his hair. "I can't let that happen. It will make things worse. And I don't have much time left to fool with these actors. I've got to link with Leon and return to the time stream at precisely the same time he does."

The LOC flashed in silence, waiting for instructions.

Noel sighed, wondering how he was going to straighten everything out. "How much time remains on this mission?"

"Thirteen hours, twenty-two minutes, forty-eight seconds."

"Then our deadline is about dawn. No, a little past. Till early morning, then."

"Affirmative."

Noel didn't want to think about what could happen when and if he ran out of time. He shook his head and punched his knee with one fist. He *wasn't* going to stay here the rest of his life. He wasn't going to let Leon trap him here.

"Can you tell me where Leon is now?"

"Negative."

"He's left?"

"Unknown."

"Oh." Noel swallowed, trying to stay calm. "You're not sensing him."

"Affirmative."

"Why not? You didn't pick up on him yesterday, either, at least not until he utilized his LOC. Is that the problem now? Are you able to only register LOC activity?"

"Affirmative."

"Why? You could register him independently before."

The LOC flashed faster, almost with agitation. "Parameters have changed," it said at last.

"What does that mean?"

"Parameters have changed."

"Explain change."

"Alteration of existing circumstances from what was before."

"Oh, that's very good," said Noel in disgust. "Cancel damping field. Unfreeze the hinges on the door. Turn yourself off."

With a final flash of blue light, the LOC complied.

Noel sat there in the wavering candlelight and considered his options. He didn't have many.

The first thing he had to do was keep the actors on track. That meant he had to convince them his wound wasn't as bad as they thought. Well, medical science was pretty primitive in this century. Maybe he could bluff his way through it.

Maybe.

He'd better make it work because he had to get to the second and far more important item on his list. And that was to capture Leon.

Noel shook his head. It wasn't going to be easy.

When Noel opened the door, Darcy and Hal jumped and whirled around to stare at him as though he were a ghost.

"Hi there," said Noel.

Their eyes widened. Hal's face turned white. He eased away. "G-got to tell Jack," he mumbled, and vanished.

Darcy stood rooted, staring at Noel as though he were completely dumbfounded.

Noel had peered at his reflection briefly. He knew his dark hair was standing on end, his breeches were torn at one knee, and the bandages tied clumsily across his chest and shoulder were black with dried blood.

"Got any food?" asked Noel. "I'm starved. How long until curtain?"

Darcy opened his mouth, but said nothing. He lifted one visibly trembling hand and touched his fingertip to Noel's bare arm. At contact, he flinched back.

Noel grinned. "Still solid. Come on, Darcy, pull yourself together. I'm not a ghost."

"You . . ." Darcy's voice came out as a squeak. He stopped, cleared his throat, and tried again. "You were dying."

Noel shook his head. "Flesh wound. Looked worse than it was. You know how they bleed. But—"

"Confound it, I've been on a battlefield before!" cried Darcy angrily. "The man put the damned knife through your lung. Men don't survive that kind of injury, and if they do, it's by the grace of God and after a long convalescence."

"I heal fast," said Noel.

Darcy stepped back and held up his hands as though to ward Noel off. "There's a devil in you."

"Now, Darcy, don't get superstitious on me," said Noel.

But Darcy's face was mottled with red. His eyes blazed with fear. "Witch!"

"That's not true. I'm—" Noel lost his breath and had to sag momentarily against the doorjamb to rest.

The sound of hurrying footsteps whipped Darcy's head around. He glanced once more at Noel and fled.

"Darcy!"

Jack came into sight, already garbed in a resplendent coat of emerald green. Crimson bows had been tied around both sleeves, and his wide petticoat breeches were peacock blue. His shoes had high red heels, and large bows adorned them as well. A small-sword hung at his side. His face had been painted very white, then rouged. He wore, of all things, a beauty patch on his cheek. He was followed timorously by a round-eyed Hal, who hung back. At the sight of Noel, Jack's hurried stride faltered. He came to a halt a healthy distance away and stared.

"Told you!" quavered Hal.

"Stay away from him, Jack," called Darcy from far down the corridor. "He's a witch."

"Nonsense," said Jack, his deep voice echoing off the walls. "Both of you keep out of the ale tonight. You've had too much already."

Ignoring their indignant protests, he walked toward Noel. "My poor fellow," he said gently, "you'll do yourself harm getting up like this. You need to rest. Let me help you back to bed."

Noel put out a hand to stop Jack from steering him back into the room. "I'm fine," he said. "Just a little wobbly, but I'll be all right as soon as I've had something to eat."

Jack laughed, but his eyes were puzzled as he said, "As hungry as ever, eh? That's a good sign, I suppose. But you're in a bad way, my boy. You must lie down again."

"No. I'll be all right," repeated Noel stubbornly. "How long till curtain?"

Consternation entered Jack's expression. "That's no longer for you to worry about. We'll manage without—"

"No!" said Noel. "I'll do my part. I gave my word. You said I—"

"I said many things this afternoon, which I now regret," said Jack. "My cursed temper gets away from me too often. I thought you were playing a game with us. But the man who stabbed you—"

"An old enemy," said Noel.

Jack blinked and looked more astonished than ever. "Your brother, more like."

It was Noel's turn to stare. "You saw him?"

"Who hasn't? He's one of the guests, a favorite of the king's. Everyone is speculating on what brought on the fight, but at least our little company knows now why you were so eager to use us to gain access to Clarendon House."

There was no point in denying that anymore. Noel said, "I still intend to do the play. I asked for the job in good faith. I hoped my . . . brother would be here tonight, but I didn't expect this." Ruefully he gestured at his bandaged chest.

"Obviously," said Jack dryly. "I think now, however, that you should return to bed. Your fever gives you the illusion of strength, but soon your weakness will conquer you again and bring you down. If you swoon and fall, you could lose the last few drops of blood you have. We had the devil's own time stopping the flow."

"I'm surprised I wasn't leeched," said Noel.

"We talked about sending for a barber, but there wasn't time with His Lordship wanting to give us our instructions for the evening. We bundled you in here and left you in God's hands. Now go and lie down like a good fellow and leave us to our work."

"Jack, listen. I know my part. I'll be able to—"

Jack gripped Noel by his arms and shoved him gently back into the room, where he pushed him into a sitting position on the cot. "You're stouthearted and you mean well, but it's not to be. After all the drama this afternoon, with ladies fainting at the sight of blood and Lady Kemble losing her diamond earrings, the lord chancellor wants light entertainment, something more appropriate for the garden setting."

Noel scowled, feeling his future sink further. "I'm sure His Lordship would do anything to avoid a political drama about betrayal at the highest levels," he muttered.

Jack blanched. "Noel, you talk treason."

Noel looked up earnestly and took the risk of candor. "The people are against Clarendon. They resent the way he's conducting the war with Holland. They resent this house and the money he's spent on it. Fifty thousand pounds to build it, while the king's bankrupt and begging. Hear me! I could wager you that in a year or so this house will be torn down by angry people, and I'd win the bet. Clarendon was a good adviser to the king in the past, but his judgment has grown corrupt."

Jack glanced uneasily at the door. "I have no part in politics. I warned you not to embroil us in any intrigues."

"Someone has to make the king see the truth about Clarendon," said Noel urgently. "You already planned to perform *Julius Caesar*. It's perfect for the purpose. Why not stick to your original plan?"

"Because we've taken His Lordship's gold, and we're bound to perform what His Lordship wants," said Jack tightly. "Will was right to doubt you from the first."

"I'm just trying to help."

"Perhaps. And perhaps you're lying again," said Jack. "Whatever your game, it's too serious for my blood. You've lost enough of yours for one day. Why don't you take the opportunity to slip out while we entertain the court? Let it go."

Noel met his eyes. "I can't."

Jack sighed. "And I cannot help you. We are going to perform two acts of *A Midsummer Night's Dream.* God keep you. Good-bye."

"Jack, wait—"

But the actor turned away. Springing up, Noel caught his sleeve.

Jack turned on him furiously. "In God's name, leave us be!" he said. "You are worse than a gadfly, stinging here and there. You damned near got us discharged this afternoon, spilling your blood all over the flagstones, and me and Will having to explain what the devil you were doing accosting one of His Lordship's guests in the first place. By God, I tell you that were you not half-dead already, I'd take my sword to you. Now you've done enough harm, and that's an end to it. We'll see no more of you."

"Jack, wait. I'm sorry. I—"

But Jack wrenched free of Noel's grip. He walked out without looking back, and Noel was left standing in the room with the taste of failure bitter in his mouth.

Even if he got near Leon again between now and morning, they had nowhere to return to.

CHAPTER 14

The late-summer twilight lingered for hours. The court sat in the soft evening air, torchlight sparking brilliant highlights in their jewels and glowing richly upon silks and satins. The play sounded like a success from the frequent sounds of laughter. Noel skulked in the shadows, watching the audience play cards and murmur among themselves. Only now and then did they pay attention to the performance, calling out remarks or making crude jokes that evoked laughter and stopped the play. To Noel's surprise the actors seemed unperturbed by these interruptions. They would shoot back retorts—entirely in character—that brought more laughter. He realized that he would have been thrown completely by this type of performing; he probably would have lost his lines and his temper both.

Right now, however, he was more concerned with his twin. Leon, who possessed the infuriating catlike knack of always landing on his feet, had already insinuated himself into the king's friendship. From his hiding place in the fragrant shrubbery Noel watched Leon nibbling comfits and guzzling wine. Now and then the king would lean over and murmur a remark in Leon's ear, and they would laugh together. Both of them had a lady on their laps. The king's companion was feeding him grapes, followed by teasing little kisses. Leon's companion had, beneath the cover of the shadows and an artful placement of her fan, let a breast slip free of her bodice.

Noel's frown deepened. With the queen not present to maintain decorum, everyone seemed to be having a splendid time, except for the host, who looked as though someone had punched him in the stomach. Lord Clarendon tried to pretend to watch the play, but his gaze strayed constantly to Leon.

Noel knew that the lord chancellor had already fallen from favor. It didn't have to be written on a sign. The king's behavior tonight, ignoring his host and pandering to Leon, made it clear. Clarendon might keep his office for a while, but Leon had cost him the king's friendship. Without that, Clarendon's political enemies would pull him down soon enough.

Which all meant that Noel's attempts to right the bobble in history had been in vain. Leon had effortlessly fixed what Noel had messed up.

Noel knew he should be grateful, but despite his relief, all he could feel was a burning resentment. It wasn't supposed to happen this way. Leon was the one who always tried to change history and destroy the future, and Noel was always the one who struggled to put everything back in place. But this time their roles had been reversed.

It seemed to prove, more strongly than ever, that Noel had become the copy.

Fresh anger boiled through him, and his hands curled into fists. He tried to tell himself it didn't matter as long as history was saved.

But it did matter; it mattered to him personally.

He couldn't face the idea of having made the sacrificial decision to reenter the past and fix the time distortion, only to have become the bad guy. Leon had always been a pest, true, but because Leon was malicious and self-serving it had been natural to hate him, natural to punish him, natural to stop his activities. Now, in some ironic twist of fate, Leon—who had lied, cheated, stolen, manipulated, and murdered his way through time—had ended up the good guy.

It made no sense, but that was the way it was.

Noel tightened his lips and shifted his position in the shrubbery. It seemed incredible that even Leon could get away with stabbing him in broad daylight in Clarendon's backyard in front of numerous witnesses, but as long as Leon thought he was dead, that gave Noel a slight advantage.

He needed every advantage he could gain, because he still intended to take Leon back to the twenty-sixth century.

While the party went on, Noel gripped the hilt of his sword. He wished Leon would act like a normal human being for once and step into the bushes to take a whiz. Then he could ambush his twin and haul him off.

But Leon remained stuck to the king's side like a leech. Noel knew if he attempted an abduction, the king's guards would have his head on a pike before he could turn around.

Wishing he had some of Leon's telepathic abilities, Noel glared at his twin from his place of concealment. "Take a walk. Your bladder must be bursting," he whispered. "Entice the woman into the shrubbery. Do *something.*"

But Leon lolled in his chair, stealing kisses, giggling, and stuffing himself with food and drink as though he had all the time in the world.

The play ended, and musicians took the actors' place. A few people commenced dancing, but the king was yawning. Noel forced himself to perk up and pay attention. If the king was tired and left, the party would have to break up.

At midnight, Clarendon rose to his feet. "Would Your Majesty care for a light supper of cold lobster and—"

"Hmm? No, thank you," said the king. "We shall be going home shortly. Direct our carriage to be ready in half an hour."

Even in the torchlight Clarendon looked pale. He bowed, struggling to keep his composure. "Of course, Your Majesty."

The king turned to Leon. "You shall join us in our carriage, Leon."

"I'm honored, Your Majesty."

The fatuous self-satisfaction in Leon's voice made Noel mouth silent curses to himself.

The king laughed and pinched the woman he'd been fondling all evening. "A little impromptu party in the moonlight, eh, my dear?"

She giggled behind her fan. "Indeed, Your Majesty. I love carriage rides best of all."

Disgusted, Noel backed away and slipped around the end of the house. He had a plan now, at least. It was desperate and foolhardy, but that hardly mattered as long as it worked.

The king's guards played dice with the grooms and coachmen in the torchlit stable yard. Noel took a moment to straighten his clothes and tip his hat to a jaunty angle.

Drawing in a deep breath, he strolled into the light with a hand on his sword hilt and a supercilious smirk on his face.

One of the grooms saw him, and scrambled to his feet hastily. "Lord Nardek," he said, tugging his forelock in respect while the others abandoned their dice and rose to attention.

"Carry on," said Noel. "I don't mean to interrupt your game. I just have some special instructions from the king—"

"You men!" said the ringing tones of one of Clarendon's footmen. "The king wants his carriage in half an hour. Look sharp!"

Seeing Noel as he came up, he stopped in obvious confusion and bowed. "Your pardon, I'm sure, Lord Nardek."

"Stay," said Noel when the man would have retreated. "You can reinforce what I say. The king asked me to convey certain private instructions for his journey home."

"Yes, my lord?"

"Uh, there are some ladies involved. A special side trip in the moonlight . . . some dawdling . . . privacy . . . that sort of thing."

The coachmen grinned and nudged each other. The captain of the guard cleared his throat. "We understand perfectly."

"Well, it sounds charming, but it's new to me," said Noel. "Since I'm invited along, I'd like to know whether I'm expected to enjoy myself while being driven fast over rough roads with a pack of mounted horsemen around me or—"

"Ahem," said the captain while the men snickered among themselves. "If the king desires, we can arrange for two coaches. The king's royal coach with his outriders will take the official route homeward, while a private coach can drive about the countryside as long as there's moonlight enough to show the coachman the road."

"But is it safe?" asked Noel. "I mean with all these highwaymen being hanged today . . ."

"Well, there ye are, sir," piped up a groom. "With 'em all 'anged, who's to rob ye?"

"I can divide my forces," began the captain, but Noel held up his hand imperiously.

"Nonsense. I quite like this idea of driving about incognito. And the groom is correct. There should be no danger at all."

"Very little, sir. Besides, His Majesty is very handy with arms."

"As am I." Noel nodded. "Very good. I think a route along the river would be pleasant."

"Yes, my lord."

"Then it's settled. Make the arrangements, Captain. I appreciate your discretion."

The captain bowed, and Noel walked away.

He kept his back straight and put a swagger in his stride, imitating Leon as best he could. But all the while he was thinking about the king's reputed prowess with weapons. He had succeeded in getting rid of the guards, but if the king or Leon shot him, his plan would still fail.

But what if I can't die? he asked himself with a sour inner flippancy.

He touched his wounded shoulder, which felt hardly sore at all now beneath the bandage. He might heal impossibly fast, but he still felt mortality hanging around his neck. He knew that if either man shot him in a vital place, he could indeed die.

Better not to think about it at all. Better to just act, because he was too desperate to play it safe now.

As soon as he reached the cover of darkness, he nipped around to the rear of the stables and plunged inside. The warm, sweaty interior was pungent with the smells of animal, oiled leather, hay, and dung. The great beasts nickered and shuffled about their stalls. Noel forced himself to move quietly so as not to alarm them, yet he couldn't dawdle now. If he was to steal a horse, he had to do so before the grooms came in to harness a team.

Murmuring soothingly to a horse, he groped around in the shadowy darkness and managed to fumble a bridle onto the animal's head. Taking a saddle off a wall hook, he held it over one arm while he coaxed the snorting horse from its stall and out the back door.

Just as he closed the door, torchlight flared inside the stables, and the grooms came in.

Startled, Noel gave a sharp tug on the reins and led his mount down the stretch of lawn toward the rear of the property.

Within the cover of a small copse of trees, he saddled the horse, his nervousness and haste making the animal fretful and hard to handle. Finally, however, he got the girth fastened snugly and swung himself up.

The horse was a tall, long-legged hunter. As soon as Noel found his stirrups and gathered the reins, the horse strode out, ears forward, head alert and tossing with eagerness to go.

Touching the pistol in his pocket for reassurance, Noel touched his heels to the horse and galloped away.

He was riding up and down along a level stretch of road a short while later, seeking a good ambush spot, when a pistol retort crashed out. His horse reared in fright, and Noel heard the pistol ball whiz by dangerously close to his head.

His heart in his mouth, he clung desperately to the reins, trying to control his mount.

A gruff voice called out, "You there! Stand and deliver!"

Still struggling with his horse, which swung around and tried to buck, Noel could make no sense of the command. "What?"

"I said to stand and deliver! Are you daft? Stick tight afore I puts the next ball right between your eyes."

It was definitely a threat, but Noel was too furious at this interruption to pay heed to the danger he was in. "Are you holding me up?"

"Aye, what do you think?"

A horse and rider emerged from the darkness beneath the trees. The moonlight revealed a man swathed in a cloak. His hat was pulled down low, and a scarf concealed his face to his eyes. He held a pistol aimed at Noel, who sat motionless on his now-calm horse.

The irony of the situation was too much.

"Damn it, man," said Noel impatiently, "I'm busy. Why don't you pick on someone else?"

"Ah, now I know that voice from somewhere," said the highwayman. He brought his horse a step closer. "It's the fellow from the Horse and Crown, the peckish one what caught my Becky's eye."

Noel stared in turn. "Robert Mallory?" he said at last, remembering the big-nosed man who'd sat beside him while he ate dinner.

The robber pulled down the scarf from his face and grinned. He tapped the side of his warty nose. "I hoped we'd meet in a business capacity one of these fine days. Been fleeced in London town yet, my friend?"

"No," said Noel shortly before he thought. "Er, that is, I haven't—"

"Oh, enough of the chatter, friend. Hand it—"

"But I didn't know you were a bandit. I thought—"

"Told you, didn't I? Played more than fair. Don't be holding a grudge now. Just—"

"But you said you were on the, um, bridle-lay."

"Aye," said Mallory impatiently. "What do ye think this is?"

"Oh," said Noel. "No one explained. I thought—"

"Never mind what you thought. Fair's fair. Hand it over like a good fellow, and I'll let you go on your way."

"Hand what over?" said Noel blankly, thinking Mallory wanted his weapons.

"Your nob, daffy!"

"My what?"

"Your nob, your bounty, your yellow coach wheels."

"Oh!" said Noel, catching on. "My money."

Mallory heaved a huge sigh. "Green as a willow branch. Yes, your money, my lad. Let's not take all night about this, eh? There's a coach coming in the distance—"

Noel whirled around as though stung. "The coach! Damn! Mallory, get out of the road. I've got work to do."

Spurring his horse forward, Mallory blocked Noel's path. "What kind of work?"

"Don't be an idiot," said Noel furiously. "What do you think?"

Mallory tipped back his head and hooted. "You? That's the best I've heard all day. You?"

"Stop laughing. You'll tip them off. This is vital. I have to stop the king from—"

"Hush," said Mallory, his laughter gone in an instant. He was close enough now for Noel to see his face, and his expression was dead serious. "Did I hear you say that's the king's coach?"

"It is," said Noel. He could hear it himself, the hoofbeats of the horses making a gentle, steady cadence in the distance. His mount's ears pricked that way.

"God in heaven, I ain't daft enough to hold up the king. For all my faults, I'm a loyal subject, and no man'll dare—"

"Oh, shut up. I'm not going to rob the king," said Noel with exasperation. "It's my . . . my brother. He's traveling in the carriage too. Look, I don't have time to explain the whole thing. But I have to get Leon in my custody."

"But, mercy on us, man, you can't hold up the *king*."

"I'm not going to hold up the king. I just want to stop him long enough to drag my brother out."

"Same thing," said Mallory primly. "Ain't done, my lad. Ain't done at all."

Noel saw the carriage come around the bend. His nerves tightened, and he drew his pistol from his pocket and trained it on Mallory.

"I give you my word I mean no harm to His Majesty. But I will stop this carriage and I will get my brother. You can help me, or get out of the way and let me do it alone."

He and Mallory stared at each other for several seconds while the coach came closer. A horn sounded for them to clear the road. Noel's nerves jumped, but he kept his gaze and his pistol trained on the highwayman.

At last Mallory broke the deadlock and glanced over his shoulder at the carriage. "It'll never work," he said. "Got out-riders for protection. They'll riddle you with holes as soon as you let off the barker."

Noel looked and saw that Mallory was right. About half of the king's guards were traveling in the wake of the carriage. "Damn," he said softly, feeling disappointment sour and cold on his tongue.

"Aw, you're daft, but you've a spirit I like," said Mallory. "Hand over your purse, and I'll help draw 'em off."

"Done," said Noel.

He drew out his money and tossed the bag to Mallory. The bandit went to work reloading his pistol.

"Stand out in the center of the road and stop 'em," he said. "I'll draw 'em off, but you'll have to work quick."

"Right." Noel nodded and tensed himself in the saddle. He couldn't seem to draw a complete breath, and his mouth was as dry as the powder in his pistol.

"Swear on the name of God and all you hold sacred that no harm'll come to the king."

"I swear before God, before my mother, and upon my honor that I mean no harm to the king," said Noel solemnly.

Mallory nodded. "That's it, then. We'll do it."

He pulled up his scarf and glared at Noel. "Have you no sense? Disguise yourself quick."

"I'm not a thief," said Noel. "It's Leon I want, nothing else."

Mallory sighed deeply. "A waste," he muttered. "The ambush of a lifetime, and naught to show for it."

"You have every penny I own," retorted Noel.

Mallory chuckled. The man sitting beside the coachman blew the trumpet again, louder, and Mallory settled himself deep in the saddle.

"This is it, my lad," he muttered. "If you must shoot, put it in the guard alongside the coachman. He's the one who'll be a danger to us."

Indeed, Mallory was right. Noel saw the guard pulling an awkward blunderbuss out from beneath the seat.

"Clear the road!" he shouted. "Let us pass!"

They were close enough now for Noel to see that the king was indeed riding in a plain, ordinary carriage, but the outriders wore royal livery. They cantered forward now.

"Stand and deliver!" yelled Mallory, standing up in his stirrups and waving his pistol.

Someone fired a shot. It whizzed between Noel and Mallory. They swung apart and headed for separate sides of the stopped carriage. As Noel rode around in front of the frightened team, the guard on the seat stood up and took aim. Noel fired his pistol, and the man toppled over, clutching his arm.

On the other side, several shots rang out. Mallory let out a whoop, and galloped away. The outriders set off in pursuit. Noel had no time to lose. Flinging himself off his horse, he gripped his emptied pistol and wrenched open the door.

A dagger flew out, missing his head by inches. Rattled by the near miss, Noel let the door bang against the side of the carriage and leaned inside. He held his pistol just inches from the king's large nose.

A lantern swayed from the silk-lined ceiling of the carriage. The king, his long dark hair hanging in his face, wore only his shirt and breeches. He half reclined on the seat with a woman who was naked to the waist.

She gave a muffled little scream and pulled up her bodice. The king was pale, but his gaze never wavered from Noel's.

"Leon," he said softly, his voice hurt, "what is this betrayal you deal us?"

"I'm not Leon. I'm Noel, his twin brother," said Noel roughly. His gaze shot around the cramped interior of the carriage again, unable to believe that Leon was not here. "Where is he? Damn it, where is he?"

The king's eyes widened. "He had other plans and did not join us. How did you overhear—"

"Never mind that," said Noel, too upset to remember who he was talking to. "Where is he now?"

The king raised his brows.

"Look, I don't have time to be polite about this. Where is he? Do you know? What kind of plans? I've got to find him."

The woman made a little movement, and the king stilled her with his hand. He said nothing in reply to Noel's questions.

With a sigh Noel raised his pistol. "I have nothing against you personally, but I have to find my brother before—"

Something heavy and unbelievably hard crashed into the back of Noel's head. His vision flared white, then red, then black, and he was gone long before he hit the ground.

CHAPTER 15

Noel awakened to the sound of thunder and a sickening sway of the world. After a few seconds, his vision cleared and he found himself staring at a moonlit, starry sky and the silhouette of tree branches passing overhead.

Flying trees? he wondered fuzzily, then realized that the thunder he heard came from pounding hoofbeats. He was lying on top of the king's carriage while it careened down the road.

The wind was cool against his flushed face. He shook his hair back from his eyes and tried raising his head. It hurt, and he was tempted to sink back into lethargy, but the night's business wasn't finished.

There were only a few hours remaining in which to find Leon. He couldn't afford to stay here—tied? yes, tied—and be thrown into the Tower or some other dungeon until they executed him in a very unpleasant way. People didn't take kindly to having their king held at gunpoint.

Noel sank back with a soft groan and mentally kicked himself. If only Leon had been where he was supposed to be . . . but when had his twin ever cooperated?

Turning his head to the right, he saw the back of the coachman, sitting tall above the bobbing backs of the horses. Behind the carriage, eating its dust, rode the guards. Noel wondered what had become of Robert Mallory. He hoped the bandit had escaped, but if he hadn't Mallory was on his own. Noel had to worry about himself now.

"LOC," he whispered. "Keep it very, very quiet."

The LOC pulsed warmly against his wrist.

"Run a check. Has history righted itself? Will Clarendon be replaced on the king's cabinet?"

"Affirmative," intoned the LOC softly.

Noel blew out his breath in relief. "Good. LOC, determine our direction heading. Are we heading into London or away from it?"

"Heading is northwest—"

"Away from London."

"Affirmative."

"I wish I knew if that were good or bad." Noel squinted at the night sky and thought a moment. "How much time remaining?"

"Four hours, thirty-two minutes—"

"Stop. Are you registering LOC activity from Leon?"

"Affirmative."

Noel nearly sat up in his excitement. "You are?" he whispered, careful to keep his voice lower than the rush of wind. "Where? What's his location?"

"London."

Noel waited a moment, but it seemed the LOC wasn't going to say anything else. He snorted. "You don't happen to have a more precise address, do you?"

"Precision is not possible under current conditions."

"On my end, or his?"

"His."

"So what's he doing? Moving around?"

"Affirmative."

"Can you give me a general area? London's a pretty big town. Or didn't you know that?"

"Square miles equivalent to—"

"Stop!" said Noel impatiently.

The driver glanced back at him, and Noel froze with his face turned away. After a few seconds, he dared cut his eye around to peek at the driver's back. The man was facing forward again.

In relief, Noel slowly eased out his breath. He had to be careful.

"LOC," he whispered cautiously. "Give me some landmark, some reference."

The LOC pulsed warmly against his wrist for several seconds. "Present landmarks do not precisely correspond with information in my data banks."

Noel pursed his lips. "That's right," he said. "I keep forgetting the city burned . . . wait a minute. What's today?"

"Sunday—"

"No, the date."

"September second, 1666—"

"September second!" said Noel. "Isn't this the day the Great Fire started?"

"Affirmative. The Great Fire of London burned for five days and destroyed more than—"

"Stop. Where did it start?"

"Scanning . . . a baker's house in Pudding Lane. The water engine in that neighborhood was out of order. Wind carried the fire to St. Paul's Cathedral—"

"Which was destroyed," said Noel.

"The East End was destroyed, then the fire spread to the heart of the city," continued the LOC. "It was considered popish arson, and Lord Clarendon was blamed."

Dark suspicions were rising in Noel. "Is my—is Leon setting this up to get rid of Clarendon?" he asked.

"Unknown."

"Is Leon in the East End right now?"

"Affirmative."

"Is he setting that fire?"

The LOC pulsed a long while. "Scanning . . . Leon's LOC activity does not register in Pudding Lane."

"But I'll bet you an entire circuit overhaul that he'll be there come dawn," said Noel grimly. "Damn, he's going to torch the city. I've got to get free."

Noel started struggling against the ropes binding his wrists.

"The Great Fire is a historical occurrence that must not change."

Noel looked up. "What?"

"The Great Fire is a historical occurrence that must not change."

Noel stopped trying to twist free of the ropes. "Yeah, you're right. That can't be it. There's only one thing you can count on from Leon, and that is he'll always try to change history. Why should he preserve it?"

"Preservation is not his pattern."

"No, although he saved our bacon tonight with that Clarendon business." Noel's puzzlement grew as he tried to reason it out. "But everything is backward this time. Inverted. We're following each other's scripts . . . which means . . ."

Noel sat bolt upright in dismay. "My God!"

The coachman looked over his shoulder. "Hey! Lie down and keep quiet, ye damned filthy traitor. Better pray God yer soul to keep afore they takes off yer nasty head."

Noel went flat, but his mind was racing. He had to be right. There was no other answer. Leon was trying to *stop* the fire from happening. That meant . . .

"I have to start it," whispered Noel aloud.

He thought about the lives that would be lost, the number of people that would be turned out of their homes, the fortunes shattered, the countless buildings that would be destroyed, a city flattened and charred, decimated more thoroughly than Hitler's bombs during the middle of the twentieth century. He didn't want the responsibility for that.

But he dared not leave it to chance, not with Leon striving to mess up the equation of history. Even if Leon filled the water engine, even if Leon pitched in to help stop the blaze just as it started—those little things could quench the fire completely.

And history would change again, leaving Noel with no future.

He set his jaw. It had to be done. He had no choice.

"LOC," he whispered. "Burn through these ropes."

The LOC did not comply.

"LOC!"

The coachman glanced back and cracked his whip across Noel's chest. "Quit yer shoutin'! Lie flat or ye'll never see a trial."

The whip stung viciously. Noel laid down again, trying to think of a means of escape. The top of the carriage vibrated and bounced beneath him as it bowled along. Through the trees lining the road, he glimpsed a reflection of silver.

It was the river. This stretch of road bordered the Thames.

He got an idea.

"LOC," he said. "I order you to comply. Burn through my ropes."

"I am not programmed to harm—"

"You are programmed to assist me. I authorize override of your non-harm programming. I must be freed. Do it!"

He smelled the acrid burning of the rope fibers first. Then came the fierce heat scorching his skin. He choked back a cry of pain, and jerked his wrists apart. The charred rope snapped, and he was free.

Without hesitation, he shed his coat and scooted across the top of the carriage on his belly. He hit the coachman from behind. The man flailed his arms wildly, but Noel pushed him off balance. He fell off the seat and went tumbling into the ditch.

A shout went up from the guards. Someone fired a pistol. Busy trying to recover the reins, Noel ducked just in time. The horses, sensing they had no driver, lengthened their stride to a full gallop. Seizing a pistol from the seat, Noel fired back. One of the riders fell, and Noel tucked the spent pistol in the waistband of his breeches. The carriage careened wildly as the team veered from one side of the road to the other. Noel, balanced precariously over the gap between the traces and the carriage, lunged for the ends of the flapping reins, managed to grab one, and nearly fell under the wheels.

He caught himself, straining his muscles, and heaved himself back to safety. The carriage veered again, so sharply two wheels lifted off the road. Noel heard a royal shout of alarm from inside, and the woman's screams.

The guards whipped their horses forward, trying to come alongside the team and slow it down, but each erratic veer of the carriage prevented them from getting in front. Noel sent up a little prayer and tried again to reach the loose rein, still flopping free, but it was too far out of reach.

He realized he could never hope to get it. Besides, if he had the reins and climbed up to the seat, he'd be a sitting target. No, he was safer down here crouched between the front of the carriage and the rear of the team. The only problem was, he couldn't control where they were going.

The wheels hit an old rut in the road, and bounced. Noel

nearly lost his hold, and felt as though every bone in his body had been jarred. At this rate, they'd turn over in the ditch in a few minutes.

There was only one thing left to do. He grabbed the whip, gathered himself, and jumped forward, managing to land on the back of one of the rear horses. The animal snorted and plunged in fright, throwing his mate off stride and causing the two forward horses to stumble and shy.

A horse and rider loomed up alongside. Clutching one of the hames for support, Noel struck out with the whip. The guard's horse reared and plunged away. Noel gave his own frightened mount a pat, then slid off its right side until his feet were balanced precariously on the narrow wooden tongue running up the center of the team. One slight loss of balance, and he would fall beneath their hooves, to be cut to ribbons in a matter of seconds. He worked himself forward inch by inch in a thunder of galloping hooves, whipping manes, and jingling harness. Hidden in the midst of the running team, he knew no one dared shoot at him now. It was probably the most dangerous stunt he'd ever pulled in his life.

Don't think about it, he told himself.

He continued to creep forward, only to lose his balance as the team veered violently to the right. Twisting, he managed to land halfway across the neck of one of the horses. The animal stumbled and slowed down, forcing the others to a confused trot.

"Now we've got him!" shouted someone.

Noel jumped onto the back of the leader. Settling himself astride horse and harness, Noel scooted close to the creature's powerful, sweat-lathered neck, and gripped his reins close to the bridle.

Just as the guards managed to ride to the front, Noel swung the whip. "Go!" he shouted.

The team bolted forward once again, leaving the surprised guards behind. Noel heard furious shouts and the neighs of horses cruelly spurred. He leaned low, urging the team faster. The mane whipped in his face, and Noel squinted hard against the wind and dust.

The horses, aware that they had guidance again, steadied into a full gallop, although they were visibly tiring. Noel knew he couldn't keep them at this breakneck pace much longer, but he didn't intend to.

As soon as the ditch beside the road flattened out, Noel yanked hard on the reins and turned them off the road.

There was a mighty crashing behind, and for an instant Noel feared the carriage would turn over. He wished he had pulled the linking pin and released the traces, but it was too late for that now.

Down through the trees they plunged, the gentle slope and soft ground making the horses plunge and stumble.

"Stop them!" came the cry. "For God's sake, he's going to drown the king in the river. Stop them!"

Noel grinned to himself and cooed to his horse.

A shot went high over their heads. The horses shied and plunged aside, almost ramming themselves into a copse of trees. Noel yanked them around and cracked the whip, sending them toward the water.

The bank leveled out close to the river, and although there were trees along the edge, they were spaced far apart. Noel weaved in and out for a few minutes more, then saw an immense thicket ahead. Already the team was slowing of its own accord. The horses blew heavily.

This was all the chance he had left.

He glanced back, and saw that the guards were riding on the off side of the carriage, away from the edge of the river. Drawing up his legs, Noel swung himself off, hit the ground with his feet faster than he had expected, stumbled, and went tumbling head over heels.

He scrambled up, hearing a rider coming. A shot missed him by scant inches, and he went hurtling down the bank and dived into the water.

Shots hailed around him, zinging into the water angrily. Noel gulped in air and dived deep beneath the surface, letting the current carry him into the middle of the river.

He stayed under as long as he dared, then surfaced cautiously to gulp more air and dive again. He couldn't see in the murky depths of the cold water, and the current was stronger than he expected. But right now that was fine. It was carrying him out of pistol range, and that was all he wanted.

∞   ∞   ∞

Finally he made it to the opposite bank, a mile or more downstream from where he had escaped the king's guards. Sodden and exhausted, Noel dragged himself out onto the grass and lay there, gasping for breath.

The cramps hit him, jolting pain down his left leg. He gritted his teeth against the agony, and all the while he was protesting in his mind.

He must be too far away from Leon. His strength was failing him again.

Leon . . . how he hated the idea of being dependent on his duplicate for anything, especially something as vital as his own health. Hunger sapped him, and even his wounded shoulder ached. Besides that, he felt bruised and sore everywhere.

When the cramp eased up, he struggled to his feet and wrung the water out of his clothes. He had kept his shoes, although swimming had been extra difficult. Now, with his linen shirt sticking to his skin, he shivered against the predawn wind.

Wind, he thought. That dry, late-summer wind that was to carry the sparks of fire across the city. He turned his face to the east, where the sky was fading from black to indigo to gray. The birds had started chirping sleepily in the trees. In the distance a cock crowed, and he heard the tinkling bell of someone's cow. Dawn was coming.

He had to hurry.

CHAPTER 16

The early-morning sun was already warm and strong against a pearly pink sky by the time Noel came riding up Pudding Lane on a stolen cob. The horse was both lazy and iron mouthed. Noel had been beating the beast with a tree switch for the past mile, trying to urge it to something faster than a bone-jarring trot. Now he let it stumble to a halt, and he looked around at the peaceful scene.

The shops and houses were modest but well kept. Flowers bloomed in window boxes. A child's wooden hoop had been left on a doorstep. Cats dozed on sunny ledges. The bustle and noise he'd encountered yesterday and the day before were absent now. Quiet lay everywhere, as though all the world were content.

Then, in the distance, he heard a church bell, and another, and another, ringing out the summons to worship across London town.

Not a soul was in sight except a woman in a clean apron and shawl, herding her brood of freshly scrubbed children to church.

"Good Sunday morn to ye, sir," she said in a friendly way.

"Wait, ma'am," said Noel. "The baker's shop, where is it?"

She pointed with a smile. "Ye'll get no bread on the Lord's day, sir. Yesterday's loaves is all sold out."

"I'll take my chances," said Noel. "Or are you the baker's wife?"

"I am," she said with pride, smoothing her apron. "Ye look a proper vagrant, sir, I must say. My husband is setting the new loaves to rise before he joins us at worship. He won't sell you a bite, but perhaps he'll give ye charity. Ye look proper done in."

"Thanks."

With a nod, she walked on.

Noel slid off the cob and limped to the shop. Bright with a green door and shutters, it seemed to have no other customers. Knocking, he looked around for some evidence of Leon, but saw no one. The street was utterly quiet save for the clucking of chickens behind someone's house, and the stamp and tail swishing of his horse.

He found the shop door unlocked. Noel walked inside to an aroma redolent of yeast and cinnamon, a fragrance that almost made him swoon with hunger. He heard voices elsewhere, male and cheerful.

Noel almost called out, then he kept quiet. On impulse he glanced around and concealed himself behind the counter.

Footsteps came closer, and he heard a door open and shut.

"Well, now, my lord," said a deep, warm voice. "I'll say it again, although it's plain as plain ye want no more thanks, but if ye hadn't stopped by this day I'd have forgot to bank my fire proper, and no mistake."

"Think nothing of it, my good man," said Leon's voice.

Noel, bent low to fit beneath the counter, heard that voice—his voice—and stiffened. He would never get used to it, no matter how often he encountered Leon. Bracing his hands on the floor to keep his balance as he crouched there, he pressed his palms hard against the wooden floor.

"Well, my lord," said the baker, "they do preach on Sundays that haste makes waste. My wife don't hold with me setting the loaves to rise on a Sunday nohow, but I have a large family and I want to get ahead. Still, forgetting my fire like that . . . it's a mercy Your Lordship came by."

"Let it be a lesson to you," said Leon, "but don't dwell on it. Go to worship and be easy in your mind."

"Yes, my lord. Thank ye, my lord. Just step out and I'll lock the door tight behind us."

Noel listened to the creak of the front door opening. He held his breath, torn between grabbing Leon now or letting them leave so that he could start the fire. He had roughly a half hour left before recall would commence. There was no guarantee that Leon would linger. In fact, he was going out the door. Without him, Noel wasn't sure recall would function. But if he betrayed his presence, Leon would surely keep him from starting the fire.

With the greatest reluctance, he held himself in his hiding place, fighting the urge to jump up. No matter what the cost, he knew he had to save history first. If he failed to find Leon again, and thus trapped himself in the past, at least the time paradox principle would not be violated. That was his first duty.

But it was hard, just the same, to be noble and self-sacrificing when the one individual who could make him whole again was walking out the door.

"Where did this horse come from?" said Leon in an odd voice. "He wasn't tied out here when I arrived."

"A horse, my lord?" said the baker. "Yours?"

"Of course not mine. Would I ride a broken-down nag like that?" said Leon sharply. "Do you have customers on Sunday?"

"No, my lord," said the baker in a pious tone. "Never."

"I think you do today," said Leon.

"As you can see, my lord, there are but the two of us standing here."

"Just so. Well, good day."

"Good day, my lord."

Something snapped in Noel. He popped up from behind the counter. "Good morning, brother dear," he called out brightly. "I can't say it's a pleasure to see you again."

Leon whirled around in startlement. His narrow face paled, then an angry flush crept up from his lace collar and stained his cheeks. "You! But . . . but I killed you. I—"

He broke off, clenching his fists, his jaw knotted with frustration.

Although maintaining a wary eye on his twin, Noel plastered a big grin on his face and crossed his arms while the astonished baker looked from one of them to the other. "I may look like something the cat dragged in," Noel said, "but I'm far from dead. As you can see."

Leon scowled. "I'll kill you again, so help me—"

"Not this time," said Noel sharply. He drew out his pistol. It didn't work, being both wet and empty of powder and shot, but Leon didn't have to know that. "It's countdown to recall. We're going together."

Leon flung up his hand. "There is no recall," he said. "I've changed history, prevented the fire."

"And I'm here to see that it starts," said Noel.

"Er, what?" said the bewildered baker.

Leon shoved him aside. "Shut up. There'll be no fire, I say. This is my town. I like it just the way it is."

"It's going to be better," said Noel. "Right now it's a stinking, pestilent hole."

Leon's smile was wolfish. His silver-gray eyes remained as cold as chips of ice. "Exactly where I belong, I think you'd say."

"Not this time. I'm taking you back. I told you that at the start."

"And I told *you* I wouldn't go."

Noel made a small gesture with the pistol and raised his brows. "Let's go look at the hearth," he said.

With a cry, Leon sprang at him. Noel was prepared for that, but he didn't expect the baker to assist in the tackle. The two of them bore him to the floor. The baker threw himself bodily across Noel, despite his struggles to roll free, and pinned him while Leon wrested the pistol from his hand.

Pressing the muzzle against Noel's cheek, Leon narrowed his eyes. There was no mercy in them. No hesitation. Only hatred and malice. Noel lay there helplessly. It was like gazing into a mirror and finding his reflection come to life.

I don't want him back, thought Noel but at the same time he felt the need like an ache. He would never be complete and whole again unless he took Leon back into the time stream and reabsorbed him. A man was two parts—good and evil—and without the evil there was nothing for his good side to prevail against, nothing to improve on, nothing to hold him together.

"Leon," he said softly.

Leon chuckled. "Are you begging me for mercy?" he mocked. "You, my sanctimonious hypocrite of a brother? How amusing you are." His smile faded. "I thought I had taught you a lesson. It seems you need another."

The baker reached out with alarm. "No, my lord!"

Ignoring him, Leon pressed the muzzle of the pistol hard into Noel's cheek. The trigger clicked and clicked again. Noel lifted his gaze to Leon's and smiled.

Leon drew back, examined the empty firing pan, and flung the weapon away with an oath. "Damn you! I'll—"

Climbing to his feet, he turned away to seize a stout rolling pin from off the counter. Noel took the chance to shove the baker aside and scramble up. This time, he tackled Leon from behind, slamming him into the counter and wringing a grunt from him.

Leon twisted like a cat before Noel could catch his arms and swung the rolling pin like a club. Noel ducked and stayed at Leon's back, managing to get a half-Nelson on him. Roaring curses, Leon kicked and struggled. Noel exerted pressure on the back of Leon's neck, and his duplicate went abruptly still.

For a second there was only the sound of their panting.

Noel blinked the sweat from his eyes, felt Leon's shoulders heave beneath his arms, and put more pressure on Leon's neck. "I'll break it if I have to."

"Damn your eyes," snarled Leon, trying to swing one of his fists back.

Noel caught it and pinned it between their bodies. "We're going together this time. I'll hold you like this for as long as it takes."

"Gentlemen, please," said the baker, hovering nearby and wringing his hands. "Can't you settle this outside like—"

"Shut up," said Noel and Leon in unison.

"Get him off me," said Leon.

Noel looked into the man's eyes. "You'd better leave."

His tone and the purpose in his gaze made the baker turn pale.

"Please, sirs, my shop, my livelihood. I—"

"Go," said Noel.

The baker scuttled out, moaning to himself, and left the shop door wide open.

"To the back," said Noel, maneuvering Leon around. "March."

Leon stiffened, but Noel tightened his hold and pushed his twin through a doorway into the rear of the shop. Small win-

dows set very high provided the only illumination. A large
brick oven and hearth dominated the small kitchen. It was very
warm inside, and the air was hazy with flour dust. Across a long
pine table, dozens of bread loaves sat plump and oiled. Flour
still coated the kneading table. Huge wooden mixing bowls
and paddle-shaped spoons were stacked to one side for later
cleaning. A pair of flies buzzed lazily through the air.

Noel coughed. "This place needs some ventilation."

"You're really going to do it, aren't you?"

Noel glanced down at the vulnerable spot between Leon's
shoulder blades. Holding Leon like this, he was aware of his
twin's taut wiry muscles, aware of the sweat trickling down the
side of Leon's face, aware of how alike physically they were,
and how different. Inside, he could feel his stomach knotting
with reluctance. He said nothing.

"You're the moral one, the good one," mocked Leon. "Do
you think you can really torch this place?"

Noel closed his eyes. He knew what Leon was doing, but it
didn't help him to resist.

"Did you meet the baker's wife and her four children?" continued Leon. "Good people. Kind, warmhearted, hardworking.
Those attributes that you value so highly. They're the very kind
of people that you want the chip-dependent dreamers of your
own time to be like."

"Yes," whispered Noel.

"So why punish these folks? Why deprive them of their
livelihood, their home, all that they have?"

Noel bit his lip but he forced himself to answer. "You know
why."

Leon's scornful laugh rang out. "Bosh! It's a lie. It always
is. Saving the future? What good is it? Did you ever stop
to think while you're so busy chasing after me that maybe a
change would give us a *better* future?"

"You can't know that," said Noel. "It's too risky."

"Anything worthwhile is risky," said Leon.

"You can't tamper with lives, with time like that. You don't
know how it might come out. Besides—"

"There would be nothing to go home to," finished Leon for
him. "God, you make me sick. How can you defend that mess
in the twenty-sixth century? What have they ever done for

you, except rope you in with rules and stupidity? Have you ever stopped to think *why* you have to keep plunging into the past? Have you, Noel?"

"I believe in—"

"You believe in nothing except yourself!" said Leon. "You can't stand the century you claim to love so much. Otherwise you'd stay. But you can't stomach it, not really. You can't wait to visit the past. It's only here that you can be yourself. We can *live*, truly live in this primitive culture. We can feel. We can do whatever we dare. We can stretch and achieve. There's hope here, Noel. There's a future. But only here. If you take us back, you cut that off. You condemn us to *nothing*. It's a waste, Noel. A waste of our talent, our abilities, our lives."

Noel tried not to listen, but Leon's words made sense. He knew only too well the problems of his own time. But he'd dedicated his life to seeking a solution to them through researching the past. He'd sworn an oath to the Institute. He'd been conditioned with an implant to keep him from going rogue and staying.

"Conditioning can be overcome," said Leon softly. "Your oath means nothing."

Startled, Noel realized that Leon was reading his mind. But how? Was it because Noel was holding him pinned? Was it because they were touching? He knew normally Leon drew energy from him. This time he had drawn energy from Leon. Perhaps . . .

"Let the fire stay out," whispered Leon in a low, compelling voice. "Let history change. We'll be rich men. I can make us rich, make us powerful. You could be like me if you tried."

Noel shoved away from him violently, sending Leon staggering into the table. Loaves tumbled to the floor.

Leon caught himself and whirled around, his face red and angry. "Why won't you listen?" he shouted.

"No," said Noel raggedly. "I won't listen to you. I'll never listen to you."

"You're a fool."

"Maybe, but I'll be damned before I become like you."

Lunging past Leon, Noel ran to the hearth and kicked open the pile of ashes. Glowing red embers spilled forth, hissing with new life as they received oxygen. Noel crouched and blew on them gently, trying to coax flame. He reached for a stick of kindling when Leon careened into him and knocked him sprawling.

The impact hurt. Noel scraped his cheek on the stone floor. Pulling himself up to his hands and knees, he turned in time to see Leon stamping on the embers with his shoes. Noel tried to tackle Leon at the ankles, but Leon danced aside. He seized the poker and swung at Noel.

Rolling desperately, Noel evaded the length of iron, which clanged loudly on the floor and struck sparks. Leon swung again and again, driving Noel across the kitchen. Scrambling, unable to gain his feet, ducking and dodging the vicious blows of Leon's attack, Noel grabbed the mixing bowls and threw them at him.

While Leon dodged them, that gave Noel time to scramble to his feet. He saw a pair of long iron tongs hanging on a peg and reached for them.

Leon brought the poker crashing down on the table between Noel and the tongs. Noel stumbled back, turned halfway, and felt the poker slam across his low back. The pain drove him to his knees. He felt as though his kidney had been crushed. The agony in his spine and low ribs made him wonder if both weren't broken. He couldn't move, couldn't pull himself up and around to continue the fight. He knew, through the gray, sickening wash of pain, that at any moment Leon would bring the poker down on the back of his skull and finish him.

But the poker dropped instead on the floor with a loud clang.

Gasping, Noel dropped one hand to the floor and propped himself enough to glance over his shoulder. He saw Leon standing behind him, white to the lips with suffering. The pain and fury in Leon's pale eyes told him that somehow they had become linked back together, at least enough to reestablish the empathic connection.

"It's starting," said Noel hoarsely.

Leon's eyes widened. He staggered back a step. "No! I won't go back."

As though on cue, Noel's LOC flashed to life on his wrist. Leon's did also. Blue light and white light pulsed in unison.

"Warning," they intoned simultaneously. "Five minutes to recall."

"No!" shouted Leon. Like someone demented, he struggled with his LOC and managed to tear it from his wrist. He flung the computer across the room, into the fireplace.

Seizing the poker off the floor, Leon staggered across the room and pounded at the ashes.

"No—"

"I'm not going back," said Leon raggedly. A cloud of ashes rose about him as he went on pounding blindly through them, searching for the LOC he intended to destroy. "I'll never go back."

"You're crazy!" said Noel in alarm. He tried to rise to his feet and nearly fell. "Don't—"

The explosion blew the fireplace apart, and the force of it sent Leon sailing through the air like a rag doll. The concussion of the blast knocked Noel back. Brick and dust rained down, and black smoke filled the room.

Noel's LOC flashed rapidly, growing warm, then hot against his skin. "Warning," it said. "Recall unbalanced. Warning. Recall unbalanced."

Dazedly Noel dragged himself to his knees and looked around. There was a loud ringing in his ears, and his balance was off so that he swayed like a drunk. The smoke made it hard to see what remained of the room. He knew it had been a small blast; otherwise, he'd be dead. He groped his fingers across his face, checking for bleeding from his nose and ears. None. He'd been lucky.

As for Leon . . .

Coughing, Noel held his hand across his nose and mouth. A blaze burned at the end of the room where the hearth had been. A crock of oil had been spilled in the blast, and when the flames reached it they shot up high and hot, cutting off Noel from the door.

There was no other way out.

Struggling for breath, his eyes stinging and watering, Noel staggered to his feet, stumbled and nearly fell again, and somehow managed to keep his balance. The pain in his back was excruciating, but he knew he could not afford to surrender to it. The heat was already too intense for comfort. He could scarcely breathe, and he could not see Leon anywhere.

"Leon!" he called, then leaned over in a fit of violent coughing. He let himself sink to the floor and crawled below the level of smoke. "Leon!"

"One minute to recall," said his LOC. "Warning. Recall unbalanced. Warning."

What would happen if recall grabbed him without Leon? He shut off the fear building inside him and concentrated on finding his twin. Without the other LOC, he wasn't sure either of them had much of a chance. But without Leon there was no hope at all.

"Leon!" he called again. "Where are you?"

A flurry of movement beneath the kneading table caught his attention. He saw his twin trying to burrow further out of sight, and crawled over until he could grab Leon's ankle.

Burned and bloody across his face and neck, his coat in tatters, his fancy lace collar a tangle of charred strings, Leon kicked furiously. "Let me go. Let me go!"

"You'll die in here!" said Noel.

Both of them were coughing. The flames had reached the ceiling now, and the old wood caught with a roar. Cinders rained down, landing on Noel's back and burning through his clothing.

Leon tried again to twist free, but he was too weak to succeed. "Better to die here than in the time stream. You—"

He could not finish for coughing.

The heat was unbearable. Noel could feel his skin drying to his cheekbones, could feel his clothing absorbing the heat. He was dripping with sweat and nearly asphyxiated, but he clung harder than ever to Leon's ankle.

"You fool!" said Leon hoarsely. "It won't work, not without my LOC—"

He glanced up and screamed. Noel looked up and saw a flaming ceiling beam crash down less than five feet from them. Fire blazed up like an inferno, and Noel recoiled from the intense heat.

"We've got to get out!" he shouted. "The whole ceiling is going to come down."

"There's nowhere to go!" Leon shouted back.

Crouching against the table legs, Noel saw that he was right. More of the ceiling fell, orange flames licking hungrily as they widened the hole overhead. He could see blue sky now through the black smoke, and the air fed the fire.

Horrified, Noel clutched Leon tighter. Leon was still screaming, but Noel no longer had the breath for it. Every inch of his lungs felt scorched. The heat was too great. He could feel his eyebrows charring. His hair smelled like it was on fire. His clothes were scorching his body.

Then the whole top of the room came hurtling down at them, orange with flame and flying cinders.

Noel froze there, knowing that Leon was right. Recall wasn't going to happen. Time had run out. He couldn't even hear his LOC now. In one more second he was going to be crisped.

Without warning, the floor beneath him dissolved—as did the ceiling, the flames, the table, the walls—and Noel was falling through a cold gray mist of nothing, falling with Leon beside him, falling into a bottomless well of the dark void.

If he screamed he could not hear it. There was nothing for his senses to cling to, no reference points at all, save Leon.

Noel reached out for his twin, seeking any means to preserve his sanity.

Leon!

Noel!

For an instant they passed through each other; for an instant they were whole, one entity, the broken halves restored to completion. Noel/Leon laughed in joy, in relief. It was good. It was right.

A swirling distortion jolted by, snagging Noel/Leon and sweeping on. Tumbled helplessly in its wake, Noel/Leon felt the separation, felt the wrenching pain of being shredded, of being wrenched in two.

"Noooo!" cried Noel.

But it was done. He tried to fight clear of the time stream, but he was bumped and tumbled in all directions. Kicking out, he found himself bounced to one side and left there while the distortion went rushing on, taking Leon with it.

Then there was darkness, and quiet, and the vast, incomprehensible expanse of infinity. He tried to think, but his mind was chaos, endless jumbles of fragmented memories without reason. If this was madness, he did not know it. If this was the end of existence, how could he comprehend it?

But through the darkness came a paler molding of form and

substance and shadow. Drawn to it, Noel passed through, back
into the normal time stream.

The mist came, beyond which he could glimpse shapes and
movement. Dazed and weary, Noel watched them for a while
before at last his mind fastened there.

Institute, he thought. Home.

He reached out.

With a bump of transference, he found himself in the hard,
clarified world of reality.

He lay with his eyes closed, not willing to face anything just
yet, needing a few more moments to pull himself together.

He could feel the hard surface beneath him, could hear muted
sounds in the distance, cries of pain, cries for help. He could
smell smoke and fire. He could hear running. There came the
steady beat of alarm.

It didn't help, he thought. I went into the past to save the
Institute from destruction, and I've come back to the same
point. No effect. The lab is still on fire. The time stream is
still collapsing. I failed.

It was very cold around him, so cold he could feel his skin
growing numb. The air conditioning must have come on, trig-
gered by the heat of the fire, or else the fire-control chemicals
were creating a strange reaction.

Noel sighed and opened his eyes, knowing he had to face
the technicians, had to face Ellis, Bruthe, and Dr. Rugle. He'd
tried his best, but he hadn't been able to hang on to Leon.

Rubbing his eyes to clear them, he pushed himself slowly
up. His injuries from the fight with Leon were gone. His throat
was no longer burning from smoke inhalation, and he no longer
felt as though he had a cracked vertebra, but he felt sore and
stiff just the same.

To his shock, however, it was not Lab 14 that surrounded
him. Instead, he saw open, rolling pastureland bordered here
and there by trees and thickets. Everything was blanketed by
a thick layer of snow. He was sitting in snow, chilling, bone-
numbing snow.

He could not comprehend it. Dazedly, he scooped up a handful of snow and tasted it. Wet and clean, it was so cold it burned
his tongue. He spat it out and looked around.

In the distance something roared. He heard a whistle and

saw a cannonball sail overhead. It hit the ground with a thud that made Noel jump.

Alarmed, Noel scrambled up and glanced wildly around. He saw men in blue-and-cream uniforms running across an open field, wearing tricorn hats and carrying muskets fixed with bayonets. The army facing them stood in orderly rows, their crimson uniforms, shining boots, and bearskin hats looking precise and deadly. Another roar of artillery went off from the hill behind the redcoats, and the men in Continental blue fell like toppled puppets.

In the distance, drums and fifes were creating a din of their own. A red, white, and blue flag—tattered and stained—fluttered on a pole held in the stalwart arms of a young boy. Officers in dark blue cloaks sat on their horses, watching the battle, dispatching messengers with fresh orders.

Noel's mouth fell open. "America?" he said aloud. "The Revolutionary War? How did I end up here?"